DAVID
and the
PHOENIX

For Elliott, with best wishes

DAVID

and

the

PHOENIX

Edward Ormondroyd
by Edward Ormondroyd

ILLUSTRATED BY JOAN RAYSOR

PURPLE HOUSE PRESS

Purple House Press
Keller, TX 76248
Visit us on the Internet at www.PurpleHousePress.com

Purple House Press is a trademark of Purple House Press, Ltd. Co.

Publisher's Cataloging in Publication Data

Ormondroyd, Edward.
David and the Phoenix / by Edward Ormondroyd; illustrated by
Joan Raysor.
p.   cm.
SUMMARY: David and his new friend, the Phoenix, fly to various
adventures and misadventures with mythical beings and an ill-
intentioned scientist, until the Phoenix realizes that its destiny calls.

ISBN   1-930900-00-7 (hardcover) ISBN   1-930900-01-5 (softcover)
[1. Friendship - Fiction.   2. Animals, Mythical - Fiction.]
I. Raysor, Joan.   II. Title.
PZ7.O635   D38   2000
[Fic] - dc21   00-104408

A Limited Edition of 250 signed books is available from
www.PurpleHousePress.com

Manufactured in the USA using acid-free paper ♻
1   2   3   4   5   6   7   8   9   10
First Edition

Author's Foreword and Dedication

David and the Phoenix was my first book. I began writing it in the late 1940s when I was a student at the University of California in Berkeley. The kernel of the story popped into my head one day as a vision of a large and pompous bird diving out of a window, tripping on the sill, and crashing into a rose arbor below. Somehow (I'm still mystified by the process) the bird became the Phoenix and the window became a boy's bedroom window. With that settled, all I had to do was invent what happened before and after.

The book was published in 1957 by Follett Publishing Company of Chicago. Its reception was quiet but warm, and it did pretty well for a first book. The trade edition went through three printings. A Sunday school magazine (whose name I've forgotten) serialized it, with illustrations by Kurt Wiese. The Commonwealth Club of California chose it for their 1957 Juvenile Book Award. Best of all, in 1958 the Weekly Reader Children's Book Club brought out its own edition, thereby ensuring a widespread audience.

Readers began to get in touch to tell me how much they liked the book. Teachers wrote to say that they read it aloud to their classes, and they would send me packets of letters from their pupils. Several classes turned it into a play and sent me photographs of some wonderfully inventive costumes. Occasionally I would be introduced to someone at a party, who would say, "Oh! Are *you* the one who wrote–?" and go on to tell me that they had enjoyed it as much as their son or daughter had.

Eventually the book went out of print – but not, apparently, out of memory. When my wife, Joan, and I moved to the country in 1975, our newspaper carrier left a note in the box: "Thank you for *David and the Phoenix*. There are lots of us Phoenix watchers out here." By now I was getting letters and phone calls like this: "I read your book when I was young, and I loved it. Do you know where I can get a copy for my son (or daughter or niece or nephew)?" This was before the Internet, and I could only suggest searching in used book stores. Later, when the Net was up and running, and booksellers began to come on-line, searching became easier – but finding didn't. Used copies were scarce and prices asked for them rose to discouraging levels.

So I was delighted when Jill Morgan recently called me to say that, as a dealer in used children's books, she was aware of the continuing demand for *David and the Phoenix* and wanted to do something about it. Her proposal was direct and audacious – to bring the book back into print by republishing it herself. And so she has, in this facsimile of the original edition; and here, under the imprint of her new Purple House Press, the Phoenix flies again!

How can I better express my thanks than by dedicating this new edition, with love and the deepest gratitude, to Jill Morgan (may your first book prosper as mine did!) and to all you readers, who for more than 40 years have kept the tale of a boy and a bird alive in your hearts.

May 16, 2000

Contents

1: *In Which David Goes Mountain Climbing, and a Mysterious Voice Is Overheard*

ALL THE WAY THERE DAVID had saved this moment for himself, struggling not to peek until the proper time came. When the car finally stopped, the rest of them got out stiffly and went into the new house. But David walked slowly into the back yard with his eyes fixed on the ground. For a whole minute he stood there, not daring to look up. Then he took a deep breath,

9

clenched his hands tightly, and lifted his head.

There it was! — as Dad had described it, but infinitely more grand. It swept upward from the valley floor, beautifully shaped and soaring, so tall that its misty blue peak could surely talk face to face with the stars. To David, who had never seen a mountain before, the sight was almost too much to bear. He felt so tight and shivery inside that he didn't know whether he wanted to laugh, or cry, or both. And the really wonderful thing about the mountain was the way it *looked* at him. He was certain that it was smiling at him, like an old friend who had been waiting for years to see him again. And when he closed his eyes, he seemed to hear a voice which whispered, "Come along, then, and climb."

It would be so easy to go! The back yard was hedged in (with part of the hedge growing right across the toes of the mountain), but there was a hole in the privet large enough to crawl through. And just beyond the hedge the mountainside awaited him, going up and up in one smooth sweep until the green and tawny faded into hazy heights of rock. It was waiting for him. "Come and climb," it whispered, "come and climb."

But there was a great deal to do first. They were going to move into the new house. The moving van was standing out in front, the car must be unloaded. David would be needed to carry things. Regretfully, he waved his hand at the peak and whispered, "It shouldn't take long — I'll be back as soon as I can." Then he went around to the front door to see what could be done about speeding things up.

Inside, everything was in confusion. Dad was push-

ing chairs and tables around in an aimless way. Mother was saying, "They'll all have to go out again; we forgot to put down the rug first." Aunt Amy was making short dashes between the kitchen and the dining room, muttering to herself. And Beckie was roaring in her crib because it was time for her bottle. David asked, "Can I do anything?" — hoping that the answer would be no.

"C'mere," Aunt Amy said, grabbing him by the arm. "Help me look for that ironing board."

When the ironing board was finally located, Mother had something for him to do. And when he was finished with that, Dad called for his help. So the afternoon wore on without letup — and also without any signs of progress in their moving. When David finally got a chance to sneak out for a breathing spell, he felt his heart sink. Somehow, in all the rush and confusion, the afternoon had disappeared. Already the evening sun was throwing shadows across the side of the mountain and touching its peak with a ruddy blaze. It was too late now. He would have to wait until morning before he could climb.

As he gazed up miserably at the glowing summit, he thought he saw a tiny speck soar out from it in a brief circle. Was it a bird of some sort, or just one of those dots that swim before your eyes when you stare too long at the sky? It almost seemed like the mountain waving its hand, as if to say that it was quite all right for him to wait until morning. He felt better then, and returned more cheerfully to the moving.

It was long after dark before the moving van drove away. Beckie crooned happily over her bottle, and the rest of them gathered in the kitchen for a late supper of sandwiches and canned soup. But David could not eat until he had found the courage to ask one question:

"May I climb the mountain tomorrow?"

Aunt Amy muttered something about landslides, which were firmly fixed in her mind as the fate of people who climbed mountains. But Dad said, "I don't see why not, do you?" and looked to Mother for agreement.

Mother said, "Well . . . be very careful," in a doubtful tone, and that was that.

You never know what you will find when you climb a mountain, even if you have climbed them before — which, of course, David never had. Looking up from the foot of the mountain, he had thought that it was a smooth slope from bottom to top. But he was discovering as he climbed that it was not smooth at all, but very much broken up. There were terraces, ledges, knolls, ravines, and embankments, one after another. The exciting part of it was that each feature concealed the ones above it. At the top of a rise would be an outcropping of strangely colored rock, invisible from below. Beyond the outcropping, a small stand of aspens would quiver in the breeze, their quicksilver leaves hiding a tiny meadow on the slope behind. And when the meadow had been discovered, there would be a something else beyond. He was a real explorer now. When he got to the top, he thought, he would build a little tower of stones, the way explorers always do.

But at the end of two hours' steady climbing, he was ready to admit that he would never reach the peak that day. It still rose above his head, seeming as far distant as ever. But he did not care now. It had been a glorious climb, and the distance he had already covered was a considerable one. He looked back. The town looked like a model of a town, with little toy houses and different-colored roofs among the trees that made a darker patch on the pattern of the valley floor. The mountains on the other side of the valley seemed like blue clouds stretching out over the edge of the world. Even the peak could not give him a better view than this.

David gazed up the face of a scarp which rose like a cliff above him — a smooth, bare wall of rock that had halted his climb. Halfway up the scarp was a dark horizontal line of bushes, something like a hedge. Apparently there was a ledge or shelf there, and he decided to climb up to it before he returned home. To scale the rock face itself was impossible, however: there were no hand or foot holds. So he turned and made his way through the grass until he reached the end of the bare stone. Then he started upward again. It was hard work. Vines clutched at his feet, and the close-set bushes seemed unwilling to let him pass. He had one nasty slip, which might have been his last if he had not grabbed a tough clump of weeds at the crucial instant.

But, oh! it was worth it. He felt like shouting when at last he reached the ledge. Truly it was an enchanted place! It was a long, level strip of ground, several yards wide, carpeted with short grass and dandelions. Bushes grew along most of the outer edge. The inner edge was bounded by a second scarp — a wall of red stone with sparkling points of light imbedded in its smooth surface.

David threw himself on the grass and rolled in it. It was warm and soft and sweet-smelling; it soothed away the hurt of his aching muscles and the sting of his scratches. He rolled over on his back and cushioned his head in his hands. The sky seemed to be slipping along overhead like a broad blue river. The breeze ruffled his hair and whispered, the bushes murmured and gossiped to each other. Even the sunlight seemed to hum to him as it laid warm hands on his face.

But there was another sound, which now and then rose above these murmurs. Then it would fade and be drowned out by the breeze. Hard to say why, but it just did not seem to fit there. David propped himself up on his elbows and listened more intently. The sound faded: he had been imagining it. No, he had not been imagining it — there it was again. He sat up. Now he noticed that the ledge was divided by a thicket which grew from the inner side to the outer. The noise, whatever it was, came from the other side of the thicket.

David's curiosity was aroused, but it occurred to him that it might be wise to be cautious. The noise did not sound dangerous, but — well, he had never been up a mountain before, and there was no telling what he might find. He dropped into a crouch and crept silently up to the tangle of bushes. His heart began to pound, and he swallowed to relieve the dryness in his throat. The noise was much more distinct now, and it sounded like — like — yes, not only sounded like, but *was* — someone talking to himself.

Who could it possibly be? Well, there was only one way to find out.

He dropped down on his stomach and carefully began to worm his way under the thicket. The branches grew very low, and the ground was full of lumps and knobs which dug into him with every movement. There were vines, too, and some prickly things like thistles, which had to be pushed out of the way without allowing their leaves to rustle. He progressed by inches, pushing with his toes, pulling with his finger tips, wriggling with the rest of his body. At last he could see light breaking through the foliage in front of him — he was nearing the other side. A bunch of leaves hung before his face. He hesitated, then pushed them aside gently, slowly — and peered out.

He thought his heart would stop.

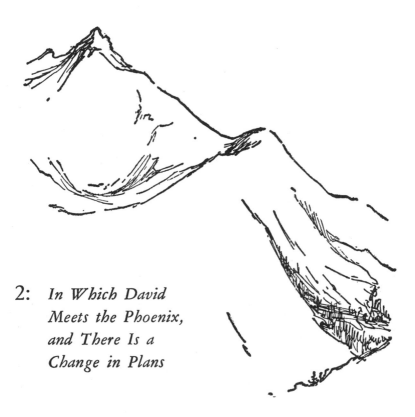

2: *In Which David
Meets the Phoenix,
and There Is a
Change in Plans*

THERE STOOD AN ENORMOUS BIRD.

David had been to the zoo, and at home he had a book
of birds with colored pictures. He knew the more common large birds of the world: the ostrich, the condor, the
albatross, eagles, cranes, storks. But *this* bird — ! Its
shape was like that of an eagle, but stouter. Its neck had
the length and elegant curve of a swan's neck. Its head

was again like an eagle's, with a hooked bird-of-prey beak, but the expression in its brown eyes was mild. The long wings were blunt at the tips, the tail was short and broad. The legs, feathered halfway down, ended in taloned feet. An iridescent sheen sparkled on its plumage, reflecting sunlight from the scarlet crest, the golden neck and back, the breast of silver, the sapphire wings and tail. Its size alone would have been enough to take David's breath away. He could have stood beneath the arch of that neck with room to spare.

But the most astonishing thing was that the bird had an open book on the ground and was apparently trying to learn part of it by heart.

"*Vivo, vives, vive,*" the bird read, very slowly and distinctly, staring hard at the book. "*Vivimos, vivís, viven. That* is simple enough, you blockhead! Now, then, without looking." It cleared its throat, looked away from the book, and repeated in a rapid mutter: "*Vivo vives vive vi* — ah — *vivi* — oh, dear, what *is* the matter with me?" Here the temptation to peek overcame it for an instant, and its head wavered. But it said, "No, no!" in a firm tone, looked carefully the other way, and began once more.

"*Vivo, vives, vive* — quite correct so far. Ah — *vi* —

ah — Oh, dear, these verbs! Where was I? Oh, yes.
Vivo — "

David's head reeled as he watched this amazing performance. There was no need to pinch himself to see if he were dreaming: he was perfectly wide awake. Everything else around him was behaving in a normal way. The mountain was solid beneath him, the sunlight streamed down as before. Yet there was the bird, unmistakably before him, undeniably studying its book and speaking to itself. David's mind caught hold of a phrase and repeated it over and over again: "What on *earth?* What on *earth?*" But of course there was no answer to that question. And he might have lain hidden there all day, staring out at the bird and marveling, had it not been for a bee which came droning into the thicket straight for him.

He had a horror of bees, ever since he had once bumped into a hive by mistake. When he heard that dread sound approaching, his whole body broke into a sweat. All thought of the bird was immediately driven from his head. He could tell from the noise that it was one of those big black-and-yellow fuzzy bees, the ones with the nasty dispositions. Perhaps — the thought paralyzed him — perhaps he was lying on its nest. On it came, buzzing and blundering through the leaves. Suddenly it was upon him, so close that he could feel the tiny breeze stirred up by its wings. All self-control vanished. He beat at it wildly with his hands, burst out of the thicket like an explosion, and smashed full tilt into the bird before he could stop himself.

With a piercing squawk the bird shot into the air, flipped over, and came fluttering down facing him — talons outstretched, hooked beak open, eyes a-glare. Completely terrified, David turned and bolted for the thicket. He managed to thrash halfway through when a vine trapped his feet. He pitched forward, shielding his face with his arms, and was caught up short by a dead branch snagging his shirt.

He was stuck. This was the end. He closed his eyes and waited, too numb with fear to think or cry out.

Nothing happened. Slowly he turned his head around. The bird, although it still glared menacingly, seemed undecided whether to attack or flee.

"What, may I ask, are you doing here?" it said at last, in a severe voice.

"I — I — I was taking a walk," David said faintly. "I'm awfully sorry if I bothered you or anything."

"You should not have come up here at *all*," the bird snapped.

"Well, I'm really sorry. But there was a bee in the bush here. I — I didn't mean to . . ." The fright had been too much. Tears started in David's eyes, and his lip began to tremble.

The bird seemed reassured, for its manner visibly softened. It lowered and folded its wings, and the glare faded from its eyes.

"I'd go away," David mumbled apologetically, "only I'm stuck." He rubbed his eyes on his sleeve.

The bird looked at his dismal face and began to fidget awkwardly. "There, there," it said. "I had no intention of — I am afraid that I — Stuck, did you say? Very easily mended, my dear fellow! Merely a question of — Here, let me look." It crashed through the thicket to where David was caught and thrust its head down through the branches. Its muffled voice came floating up. "Take heart! There seems to be — aha! just so — One moment, please — bit of vine — *there* we are!" There was a snapping sound from below, and David's foot was released. He unstuck the snag from his shirt, pushed his way out of the thicket, and sat down weakly on the grass. Whew! At least the bird was not going to harm him. It seemed to be quite a kindly creature, really. He had just frightened it and made it angry by bursting out of the bushes so suddenly.

He heard a flailing in the thicket, followed by the bird's anxious voice: "Hello! Are you still there?"

"Yes. What — ?"

There were more sounds of struggle. "This is rather awkward. I — the fact is, I am afraid, that I am stuck myself. Could you — "

"Yes, of course," said David. He smiled to himself, a little shakily, and re-entered the thicket. When he had disentangled the bird, the two of them sat down on the grass and looked at each other. They hesitated, not quite sure how to begin.

"I trust," said the bird at last, "that you are not of a scientific turn of mind?"

"I don't know," said David. "I'm interested in things, if that's what you mean."

"No, it is not. There is a great deal of difference between the interest shown by normal people and the obsessive interest of scientists. You are not, I hope, acquainted with any scientists?"

"No."

"Ah," said the bird, with a relieved sigh. "Everything is quite all right, then. I do hope that you will forgive my behavior. I am not usually so rude. The fact is that you gave me quite a horrible start."

"Oh, I'm sorry I frightened you."

"Frightened, my dear fellow?" said the bird testily. "I am never frightened. I do not know the meaning of the word."

"What I mean is," David said quickly, "that you frightened *me.*" This seemed to pacify the bird; and

David, to heighten the good impression, added: "Golly, you looked fierce."

The bird smiled complacently. "I *can* rise to a terrifying ferocity when aroused. A noble strain of fighting blood courses through my veins. Not that I go out of my way to seek quarrels, you understand. On the contrary. 'Peaceful' could well describe my general attitude. Meditative. I am usually to be found Thinking. I have a powerful intellect. No doubt you have noticed the stamp of genius on my brow."

David supposed that the bird meant its scarlet crest, and he nodded. "That's one of the first things I noticed about you."

"Indeed?" cried the bird delightedly. "You are certainly more alert than most! But, as I was saying, I am usually to be found Thinking. The first condition of Thinking is solitude. And that, I fear, is a desideratum most difficult of realization."

"I beg your pardon?"

"People," explained the bird, "do not leave you alone."

"Oh," said David. He flushed, thinking that the words had been aimed at him, and began to get up. But the bird signaled him to remain where he was.

26

"I do not mean *you*, my dear fellow. I assure you that I am delighted to make your acquaintance. It is all the others. Do you know that I have spent the greater part of my life being pursued? I was chased out of Egypt like a common game bird. Out of the mountains of Greece, too. The hills of Lebanon, the desert of Africa, the Arabian wilds — no matter where I fled, people would come prying and peering and sneaking after me. I have tried Tibet, China, and the steppes of Siberia — with the same result. At last I heard of a region where there was peace, where the inhabitants let each other alone. Here, I thought, I should — "

"Pardon me for interrupting. Where?"

"Why, *here*, to be brief," said the bird, waving its wing toward the valley. "Here, I thought, I should be able to breathe. At *my* age one likes a little quiet. Would you believe that I am close to five hundred years old?"

"Golly!" said David. "You don't look it."

The bird gave a pleased laugh. "My splendid physical condition *does* conceal my years. At any rate, I settled here in the hope of being left alone. But do you think I was safe?"

David, seeing that he was supposed to answer no, shook his head.

27

"Quite right," sighed the bird. "I was not. I had been here no more than three months when a Scientist was hot on my trail. A most disagreeable fellow, always sneaking about with binoculars, a camera, and, I fear, a gun. That is why you startled me for an instant. I thought you were he."

"Oh," David cried, "I'm awfully sorry. I didn't bother you on purpose. It's just that I never saw a mountain before, so I climbed up here to see what one looked like."

"You climbed up here?"

"Yes."

"Climbed," said the bird, looking very thoughtful. "Climbed . . . I might have known . . . It proves, you see, that the same thing could be done again by someone older and stronger. A very grave point."

"Oh, I see," said David. "You mean the — "

"Precisely! The Scientist. He is, I fear, very persistent. I first noticed him over there" — the bird waved its wing toward the opposite side of the valley — "so I removed to this location. But he will undoubtedly continue his pursuit. The bad penny always turns up. It will not be long before the sharp scientific nose is again quivering in my direction."

"Oh, dear, that's terrible!"

"Your sympathy touches me," said the bird huskily. "It is most unusual to find someone who understands. But have no fear for me. I am taking steps. I am preparing. Imagine his disappointment when he arrives here and finds me flown from the nest. I am, to be brief, leaving. Do you see this book?"

"Yes," said David. "I heard you reading it, but I couldn't understand it. Is it magic?"

"No, my boy, it is Spanish. I have chosen a little spot (chilly, but isolated) in the Andes Mountains. South America, you know. And of course one must be prepared. I am learning Spanish so that I shall be able to make my way about in South America. I must admit my extreme reluctance to depart. I have become very fond of this ledge. It is exactly suited to my needs — ideal climate, magnificent view . . ."

They fell into a lengthy silence. The bird gazed sadly out over the valley, and David rested his chin in his hands and thought. The mystery was clearing up. The bird's presence on the mountain and the fact that it had been reading a book were explained. And so natural was its speech that David found himself accepting it as nothing unusual. The thing that worried him now was that the bird would soon leave. Here they had only just met, and already the promise of a most interesting friendship was dissolving. The bird had taken time to talk to him and explain things to him as though he were an equal. And although he did not understand many of the long words it used, he felt pleased at being spoken to as though he did understand. And the bird knew all about faraway countries — had visited them and lived in them and had adventures in them for almost five hundred years. Oh, there were so many things David wanted to know and ask about! But the bird was leaving. If only he could persuade it to stay, even for a short while! He could try, anyhow — after all, the bird had said itself that it did not want to go.

"Bird — " He stopped, and flushed. It was hard to put into words.

"Your servant, my boy."

"Well — I — I don't believe I know your name," David stammered, unable to get the real question out.

"Ah, forgive me!" cried the bird, jumping up. "Permit me the honor of presenting myself. I daresay my name is familiar to you, celebrated as it is in song and story. I am the one and only, the Unique, Phoenix." And the Phoenix bowed deeply.

"Very glad to meet you," said David. "I'm David."

"Delighted, my dear fellow! An honor and a pleasure." They shook hand and wing solemnly. "Now, as you were saying — ?"

"Well, Phoenix, I was just thinking," David stammered. "It's too bad — I mean, couldn't you — it would be nice if we — Well, do you really *have* to go to South America? It would be nice if you'd stay a while, until the Scientist shows up, anyway — and I like talking with you . . ." His face burned. It seemed like a lot to ask.

The Phoenix harrumphed several times in its throat and shuffled its feet. "Really, I cannot tell you how — how much you — well, really — such a delightful request! Ah — harrumph! Perhaps it can be arranged."

"Oh, Phoenix!" David threw his arms around the bird's neck and then, unable to restrain himself any longer, turned a somersault on the grass.

"But for the present, it seems to be getting late," said the Phoenix. "We shall talk it over some other time and decide."

"Golly, it *is* late — I hadn't noticed. Well, I'll have to go, or they'll worry about me at home. But I can come up and see you tomorrow, can't I?"

"Of course, my boy! In the bustle of morning, in

the hush of noon, in the — ah — to be brief, at any time."

"And I'll bring you some cookies, if you like."

"Ah," said the Phoenix, closing its eyes. "Sugar cookies, by any chance?" it asked faintly. David noticed the feathers of its throat jumping up and down with rapid swallowing motions.

"I'll ask Aunt Amy to make some tonight."

"Ah, splendid, my boy! Splendid! Shall we say not more than — ah — that is, not *less* than — ah — fifteen?"

"All right, Phoenix. My Aunt Amy keeps a big jar full of cookies, and I can have as many as I like."

The Phoenix took David's arm, and together they strolled to the other end of the ledge.

"Now, don't mention this to anyone, but there is an old goat trail down this side. It is somewhat grown over, but eyes as sharp as yours should have no trouble with it. It will make your travels up and down easier. Another thing — I trust you will not make known our rendez-vous?"

"Our what?"

"You will not tell anyone that I am here?"

"Oh, no. I won't say a word! Well, I'll see you tomorrow."

"Yes. As the French so cleverly say it — ah — well,

to be brief, good-by, my boy. Until tomorrow, then."

David waved his hand, found the goat trail, and started down. He was too happy even to whistle, so he contented himself with running whenever he found a level place. And when he reached home, he stood on his hands in the back yard for two whole seconds.

3: *In Which It Is Decided
that David Should Have
an Education, and an
Experiment Is Made*

NEXT DAY IT TOOK LESS
than an hour to reach the ledge, and David was sure that
he could shorten the time even more when he was familiar
with the goat trail.

The Phoenix was not in sight when he arrived, and
for an instant David was stricken with fright. Had the
bird gone in spite of its promise? But no — he heard a

34

reassuring noise. It came from the thicket, and it sounded very much like a snore.

David smiled to himself and shouted, "Hello, Phoenix!"

There was a thrashing sound in the thicket, and the Phoenix appeared, looking very rumpled and yawning behind its wing.

"Greetings, my boy!" it cried. "A splendid morning!" Then the Phoenix caught sight of the paper bag in David's hand, and swallowed in a suggestive way.

David thrust the bag of cookies behind his back. "Now, Phoenix," he said firmly, "you have to promise me you won't go away to South America. You said last night that it could be arranged, so let's arrange it right now. Until we do, not one."

The Phoenix drew itself up indignantly. "My very dear fellow," it said, "you wound me. You cut me to the quick. I will not be bribed. I — " It stopped and swallowed again. "Oh, well," it continued, more mildly, "one does not fight fate, does one? I suppose under these circumstances, I must accept."

"It's settled, then!" David cried joyfully.

So they sat down on the grass together, and for a long time nothing was heard but sounds of munching.

"My boy," said the Phoenix at last, brushing the crumbs from its chest, "I take a modest pride in my way with words, but nothing in the language can do these — ah — baked poems justice. Words fail me."

"I'm glad you like them," David said politely.

"And now, my boy," continued the Phoenix, as it settled back comfortably, "I have been thinking. Yesterday you showed an intelligent interest in my problems and asked intelligent questions. You did not scoff, as others might have done. You have very rare qualities."

David flushed, and mumbled denials.

"Do not be so modest, my boy! I speak the truth. It came to me that such a mind as yours, having these qualities, should be further cultivated and refined. And I should be avoiding my clear-cut duty if I did not take this task in hand myself. Of course, I suppose some attempt to educate you has already been made, has it not?"

"Well, I go to school, if that's what you mean. Not now, though, because it's summer vacation."

"And what do they teach you there?"

"Oh, reading and writing and arithmetic, and things like that."

"Aha!" said the Phoenix triumphantly. "Just as I suspected — a classical education. Understand me — I have nothing against a classical education as such. I realize that mathematics, Greek, and Latin are excellent for the discipline of the mind. But in the broad view, a classical education is not a true education. Life is real, life is earnest. One must face it with a *practical* education. The problems of Life, my dear fellow! — classical education completely ignores them! For example, how do you tell a true Unicorn from a false one?"

"I — I don't know."

"I thought not. Where do you find the Philosopher's Stone?"

"I don't know."

"Well, then, I shall ask a simple one. What is the first rule of defense when attacked by a Chimera?"

David squirmed uncomfortably. "I'm afraid I don't know that, either," he said in a small voice.

"There you are!" cried the Phoenix. "You do not have a true, practical education — you are not ready for Life. I, my boy, am going to take your education in hand."

"Oh," said David. "Do you mean — are you going to give me — lessons?" Through his mind flashed a picture of the Phoenix (with spectacles on its beak and a ruler in its wing) writing out sentences on a blackboard. The thought gave him a sinking feeling. After all, it was summer — and summer was supposed to be vacation time.

"And what an education it will be!" the Phoenix went on, ignoring his question. "Absolutely without equal! The full benefit of my vast knowledge, plus a number of trips to — "

"Oh, *traveling!*" said David, suddenly feeling much better. "That's different. Oh, Phoenix, that'll be wonderful! Where will we go?"

"Everywhere, my boy!" said the Phoenix, with an airy wave of its wing. "To all corners of the earth. We shall visit my friends and acquaintances."

"Oh, do you have — "

"Of course, my boy! I am nothing if not a good mixer. My acquaintances (to mention but a few) include Fauns, Dragons, Unicorns, Trolls, Gryffins, Gryffons, Gryffens — "

"Excuse me," David interrupted. "What were those last three, please?"

"Gryffins," explained the Phoenix, "are the small, reddish, friendly ones. Gryffons are the quick-tempered proud ones. Gryffens — ah, well, the most anyone can say for them is that they are harmless. They are very stupid."

"I see," said David doubtfully. "What do they look like?"

"Each looks like the others, my boy, except that some are bigger and some are smaller. But to continue: Sea Monsters, Leprechauns, Rocs, Gnomes, Elves, Basilisks, Nymphs — ah — and many others. All are of the Better Sort, since, as I have many times truly observed, one is known by the company one keeps. And your education will cost you nothing. Of course it *would* be agreeable if you could supply me with cookies from time to time."

"As many as you want, Phoenix. Will we go to Africa?"

"Naturally, my boy. Your education will include — "

"And Egypt? And China? And Arabia?"

"Yes. Your education will — "

"Oh, Phoenix, Phoenix!" David jumped up and began to caper, while the Phoenix beamed. But suddenly he stopped.

"How are we going to travel, Phoenix?"

"I have wings, my boy."

"Yes, but I don't."

"Do not be so dense, my dear fellow. I shall carry you on my back, of course."

"Oh," said David weakly, "on your — on your back. Are you sure that — isn't there some other — I mean, can you do it?"

The Phoenix drew itself up to its full height. "I am hurt — yes, deeply hurt — by your lack of faith. My magnificent build should make it evident that I am an exceedingly powerful flyer. In the heyday of my youth I could fly around the world in five hours. But come along. I shall give you proof positive."

David reluctantly followed the Phoenix to a spot on the edge of the shelf where there was a gap in the bushes. He glanced over the brink. The sheer face of the scarp fell away beneath them, plunging down to the tiny trees and rocks below. He stepped back quickly with a shudder.

"Let's — let's do it tomorrow," he quavered.

"Nonsense," said the Phoenix firmly. "No time like the present. Now, then, up on my back."

"H-h-how am I going to sit?"

"On my back. Quite so — now, your arms around my neck — your legs *behind* my wings, please — there we are. Ready?"

"No," said David faintly.

"Splendid! The proof is to be demonstrated, the — to be brief, we are off!"

The great wings were outstretched. David gulped, clutched the Phoenix's neck tightly, and shut his eyes. He felt a hopping sensation, then a long, sickening downward swoop that seemed to leave his stomach far behind. A tremendous rush of air snatched at his shirt. He opened his eyes and choked with fright. The ground below was rushing up to meet them, swaying and revolving. Something was terribly wrong. The Phoenix was breathing in hoarse gasps; its wings were pounding the air frantically. Now they had turned back. The scarp loomed before them, solid and blank. Above them — high above them — was the ledge. It looked as though they would not get back to it.

Up . . . up . . . up . . . They crawled through the air. The wings flapped wildly, faster and faster. They were gaining — slipping back — gaining again. The Phoenix sobbed as it stretched its neck in the last effort. Fifty feet . . . twenty feet . . . ten . . . With a tremendous surge of its wings, the Phoenix managed to get one claw over the edge and to seize the branch of a bush in its beak. David's legs slipped from the bird's back. He dangled over the abyss from the outstretched neck, and prayed. The bush saved them. They scrabbled up over the edge, tottered there for an instant, and dropped on the grass.

For a long time they lay gasping and trembling.

At last the Phoenix weakly raised its head. "Puff —

well, my boy — puff puff — whew! — very narrow squeak.
I — puff — "

David could not answer. The earth reeled under him
and would not stop no matter how tightly he clutched the
grass.

"Puff — I repeat, I am — puff — an exceedingly
powerful flyer. There are few birds — none, I daresay —

who — puff — could have done even this much. The truth of the matter is that you are a lot — puff — heavier than you look. I hope you are not being overfed at home?"

"I — I don't know," said David, wondering whether or not he was going to be sick.

"Well, my course is clear," said the Phoenix firmly. "I must practice. Setting-up exercises, roadwork, and what not. Rigorous diet. Lots of sleep. Regular hours. Courage, my dear fellow! We shall do it yet!"

And so for the following week the Phoenix practiced.

Every morning David climbed up to the ledge, bringing sandwiches for himself, cookies for the Phoenix, and a wet towel. Then, while he kept count, the Phoenix did setting-up exercises. After this, the bird would jog trot up and down the ledge and practice jumping. Then there would be a fifteen-minute rest and refreshment period. And when that was over, the Phoenix would launch itself into the air. This was the part David liked best. It was a magnificent sight. The Phoenix dashed back and forth at top speed, wheeled in circles, shot straight up like a rocket — plunged, hovered, looped — rolled, soared, fluttered. Now and then it would swoop back to the ledge beside David and wipe the sweat from its brow.

"I trust you see signs of progress, my boy?"

David would wrap the wet towel around the Phoenix's neck. "You're doing better and better, Phoenix. I especially like that part where you twist over on your back and loop and plunge, all at the same time."

"I do perform that rather well, don't I? It is not easy. But just the thing for acquiring (ouch!) muscle tone. Are there any more cookies? Ah, there are. Delicious! As I was saying, let this be a lesson to you, my boy. If at first you don't succeed, try, try again."

The Phoenix would take wing again. And David would settle back against a rock and watch. Sometimes he thought of the education he was to get. Sometimes he thought how nice it would be if *he* could fly. And sometimes he did not think at all, but just sat with his eyes half shut, feeling the sunlight on his face and listening to the rustle of the wind in the thicket.

At the end of the week the Phoenix, after a brilliant display of acrobatics, landed on the ledge, clasped its wings behind its back, and looked solemnly at David.

"Well, my boy," it said, "I believe your education can begin forthwith. Are you ready?"

4: *In Which David and the
Phoenix Go To Visit
the Gryffins, and a
Great Danger Is
Narrowly Averted*

A CHILL RACED UP AND
down David's spine as he got to his feet.

"Do — do you think a week's practice is enough?"

"Absolutely, my dear fellow. I am now in the very
pink of condition. Not that I was ever out of condition,
mind you. It was merely that I — ah — well, to be brief,
my boy, I am now ready."

"Yes, but — well, you remember the last time."

"Yes. Look here — if it will make you feel better, suppose we have a trial flight along the ledge."

"Well — all right."

David got up as before on the Phoenix's back. The Phoenix spread its wings and hopped into the air. They glided easily down the length of the ledge, clearing the thicket in the middle by a good two feet.

"There you are, my boy," said the bird proudly, as they landed at the other end. "Shall we go?"

"Let's go," said David, as bravely as he could.

They were in the air again. Once more he felt that rush of wind against his face and heard the pounding of wings. But this time there was no giddy downward swoop. He breathed again and opened his eyes. The world was falling away, and everything on it was growing smaller by the second. The valley could be cradled in two hands; the mountains on either side looked like wrinkles in gray cloth. Now he could see plains in the distance, and little silver threads of rivers. As he looked, the whole world began to revolve slowly. The Phoenix was soaring in a wide circle.

"Well, my boy," it called over its shoulder, "who shall we visit first?"

46

"It's really up to you, Phoenix," David shouted back, "but how about the — the — Biffens or Whiffens, or whatever you called them?"

"You mean the Gryffins, Gryffons, and Gryffens, my boy? Very well. We shall visit the Gryffins only, however. It is best to leave the others alone."

The Phoenix swung around and began to fly toward the morning sun with such tremendous speed that David had to crouch down to avoid being blown off. The wind screamed past his ears, tore at his shirt and hair, and made his eyes brim over with tears. It was cold, but he was too excited to care. Below them, plains, rivers, forests, and cities rushed across the face of the earth.

"This is wonderful, Phoenix!" David shouted.

The Phoenix's reply was not clear. ". . . normal speed . . . air stream . . . prime days of my youth . . ." were the only words David caught, but he could tell from the tone that the Phoenix was pleased.

The view below was not to last long. Within half an hour they had run into a heavy overcast, and for a long time it was like flying through very wet, cold cotton. David glanced down, hoping to see the fog thin out. Suddenly he caught sight of a black object rocketing up toward them. Before he could call out a warning, the thing hurtled by, so close that its backwash very nearly knocked him from the bird's back. The Phoenix reduced speed; and the black object, after banking in a wide curve, came cruising up alongside. David was amazed to see that it was a pale but beautiful lady, dressed all in black, sitting on a broom.

"Hello, Phoenix!" she cried in a teasing voice. "I haven't seen you in *ever* so long."

"Good morning, I am sure," the Phoenix replied stiffly, staring straight ahead.

"Phoenix," the lady continued coaxingly, "I'm awfully bored. Won't you race me? Please?"

"Idle hands find mischief to do," said the Phoenix severely. "*We* are making good use of our time, and I suggest that *you* do the same."

"Don't be so stuffy, Phoenix." She pouted. "Come and race with me. I've got a new broom, and I want to see how good it is. Please!"

"No," said the Phoenix sharply.

"Oh, all right for *you!*" she said, tossing her head. "You just don't dare, because you know I'll beat your tail feathers off!" And she shot back into the mist below.

"Indeed!" the Phoenix snorted. "Beat my tail feathers off! Ha!"

"Is she a Witch?" David asked.

"Yes, my boy, and a shocking example of the decline of the younger generation. She will come to no good end, believe me. Tail feathers, indeed!"

Just then they burst out of the clouds and into the hot sunlight. Below them, the land was wild and desolate, a vast rolling plain covered for the most part with dry, tawny grass. Here and there were groves of trees drooping beneath the sun. The Phoenix, still snorting indignantly to itself, dropped to within a hundred feet of the ground. They began to soar back and forth.

"Can you see anything, my boy?"

David had never seen a Gryffin, of course; so he was not sure what to look for. But he caught sight of something lying in the shade of a bush and pointed it out to the Phoenix.

"Ah, quite so," the Phoenix said doubtfully. "It does not look like a — but we can take a closer look."

They landed and walked toward the bush. In its shadow sprawled a very untidy animal. Its tail and hindquarters were exactly like those of a panther, its chest and forelegs were like a hawk's, and it had pointed wings. Burrs matted its dusty fur. Its claws were shabby and split, and numerous black flies were crawling over its haunches. The bush trembled with its snoring.

"Bah! We are wasting our time here, my boy. This is a Gryffen. A disgusting brute, isn't it?" And the Phoenix sniffed disapprovingly.

"Maybe if we wake it up," David suggested, "it could tell us where the other ones live."

"Next to impossible. For one thing, a cannon could

not awaken the beast. For another thing, it would not, even if awake, be able to tell us anything. You simply cannot imagine the stupidity of these brutes."

"Well, let's *try* it, anyway," David said.

"Very well, my boy. But it will be a complete waste of time." The Phoenix shrugged its shoulders, stepped up to the Gryffen, and kicked it violently.

"Phoenix!" David cried in alarm. "Don't hurt it!"

"No fear," said the Phoenix, delivering another lusty kick. "One simply cannot damage a sleeping Gryffen. Give me a hand, my boy."

David took hold of the Gryffen's wing, and the Phoenix seized its tail. For the next ten minutes they kicked and pulled and pounded, shouting "HEY!" and "WAKE UP!" at the top of their lungs. It was hot work, and David finally admitted to himself that the Phoenix had been right. But before he could say so, the Phoenix completely lost its temper and savagely bit the Gryffen's tail.

That did it. The Gryffen opened one eye halfway and said, "Unffniph?"

"GET UP!!" the Phoenix bellowed.

The Gryffen struggled into a sitting position and yawned a tremendous and noisy yawn. Then it squinted

blearily at David and murmured, "What day is it?"

"Wednesday," David said. "Could you please tell us —"

"Oh, Wednesday," said the Gryffen. It thought about this for a while, mumbling "Wednesday . . . Wednesday . . ." to itself. It lifted one leg as if to scratch the fly bites, changed its mind in mid-gesture, and dropped the leg again. "Oh, *Wednesday*," it said at last. "So it isn't Saturday?"

"No," said David. "What we want to know is — "

"Not Saturday," said the Gryffen, sinking down to the ground with a huge sigh of relief. "Ah! Come back on Saturday. Saturday afternoon. I generally get up on Saturday . . . in the . . . afternoon . . ." The words faded into a snore.

"There you are, my dear fellow," said the Phoenix. "Just as I said. Oaf! Boor!"

"A *very* annoying animal," said David angrily.

"I agree, my boy. But the Gryffins are different, I assure you. Now, let me see. Where should we look — "

"There they come!" David cried suddenly. "Look!" And indeed, a number of winged creatures were loping down a hillside toward them.

"Good heavens!" the Phoenix shouted. "Those are the ones we do *not* want to meet! On my back, *quick!*"

"What are they?" David gasped as he threw himself on the bird's back.

"Gryffons!"

The Phoenix rushed along the ground a few feet and sprang into the air. But it was too late. The foremost Gryffons, with powerful strokes of their wings, shot up to meet them. The Phoenix swerved sharply. They missed the snapping beak of the first Gryffon by half an inch and dodged the second — only to smash into a third.

David was stunned by the blow and the fall. When he regained consciousness, he found himself in the tight grip of two Gryffons. The Phoenix was struggling feebly with another, and still more were crowding around them, screaming like hawks.

They looked like the sleeping Gryffen, but were as large as ponies. Their eyes were yellow and unblinking, and their tails twitched like an angry cat's. Their smell, like the lion house in the zoo, made David feel faint.

"Well, Phoenix," said the largest Gryffon coldly, "you know the Rule, I believe?"

The Phoenix smiled weakly and cleared its throat. "Ah, there, Gryffon," it said unsteadily. "Fancy meeting you here. Ah — ah — rule? What rule?"

"Rule 26," said the Gryffon. " 'No human being shall be allowed to enter the — ' "

"Oh, that rule," said the Phoenix, with a careless laugh. "I thought everyone knew that the Council of 1935 had changed it. Can it be that you have not yet heard?"

"That won't do, Phoenix. You have also heard, of course, of the penalty for breaking the Rule, which you must suffer along with this human boy?"

54

"Now, one moment, my dear Gryffon! I — ah — "

"Death!"

The Phoenix quailed, and David's legs went limp under him. But they had no chance to plead with the Gryffons. Their captors formed two lines, one on each side of them, and at a scream of command from the leader, all began to march. The Gryffon that had been holding the Phoenix winked horribly at David and made a throat-cutting gesture with its wing.

"Courage, my boy," the Phoenix whispered. "It is always darkest before dawn."

Presently they reached a hillside. David and the Phoenix were marched up to a cave and thrown in. Two of the Gryffons sat down at the entrance to guard them while the others went off to consider the best method of carrying out the penalty.

David was terribly frightened now, but he did not want to let the Phoenix know it. In a voice which trembled a little he asked, "What are we going to do?"

The Phoenix frowned. "Do not be downcast, my boy. My brain is equal to any occasion. I shall Think. Silence, please."

And the Phoenix, covering its eyes with one wing, Thought.

To keep himself occupied, David explored the cave. But there was nothing to see. The cave was small and bare. He tested the walls thoroughly to see if there were any places where they might dig their way out. There were none. His feet raised a cloud of fine dust, which got into his eyes and nose and made him sneeze violently. Discouraged, he went back to the Phoenix and sat down. There was a long silence.

Gradually an idea came to David. It started as a small, faint thought at the back of his mind, wavered, began to grow and expand and fill out — became bigger and clearer and better and —

"Phoenix!" cried David, jumping to his feet.

"My boy, my very dear boy," said the Phoenix, its voice breaking with emotion, "I have Thought, I have Pondered, I have — well, to be brief, it is no use. Stiff upper lip, my boy! We are Doomed."

"Phoenix, I — "

"Let this be a lesson to you, my boy, even though it be your last one. Fools rush in where angels fear to tread. Ah! who could have said, in the golden days of my youth, that I should come to such an end! Oh, miserable bird! Oh, unhappy boy!"

"Phoenix — "

"But we can show them how to die, my boy! We still have that — the last magnificent gesture. Let those who have lived wisely and well show that they can die in the same way! I hope I am to go first, so that you may have an example to follow."

"*Phoenix!*"

"My boy?"

"Listen, please!" And David whispered in the Phoenix's ear.

The plan had seemed like a good one while it was still in his mind, but put into words it sounded a little too simple. As he whispered, David began to feel more and more foolish, so that finally he stopped altogether.

"I — I guess it's really kind of silly," he stammered.

But the Phoenix was looking at him with hope and admiration in its eyes. "My very dear chap," it said solemnly, "I salute you. I humbly await your signal."

"Do you really think it will work?"

"My boy, it must — it can — it shall. Proceed."

Poor as the plan now seemed to David, he prepared to carry it out. Holding his breath so as not to sneeze again, he scooped up as much dust as he could hold in two hands. Then he took his position on one side of the cave, nodded the Phoenix toward the other, and glanced out to see if the guardian Gryffons were looking. They were not. "Now," he whispered.

The cave rocked with their uproar. David screamed at the top of his voice and kicked the walls. The Phoenix let out a series of ear-splitting whistles and squawks and beat its wings frantically. Echoes bounced from wall to wall. The two Gryffons came rushing into the cave, adding to the racket with their shrieking. "Now!" David shouted, and he flung the double handful of dust into the Gryffons' faces. Instantly they were all choking and sneezing in the thick cloud. He plunged between the legs of the two Gryffons, who in the confusion began to bite and tear savagely at each other.

David and the Phoenix burst out of the cave together. The other Gryffons, aroused by the noise, were bounding toward them. David flung himself on the Phoenix's back and shouted "Fly!" and sneezed. From somewhere behind him a set of talons snatched out and ripped through the back of his shirt. He kicked blindly and felt his foot crunch into something which shrieked. "Fly, Phoenix!" he sobbed. The Phoenix was already in the air and needed no encouragement. They heard raucous cries and the thunder of wings behind them. David looked back over his shoulder. The Gryffons were rising

from the ground in pursuit, their legs drawn up under them and their wings beating. "Faster!" he screamed.

"You have seen nothing in the way of flying until now, my boy," the Phoenix shouted back. "Watch this!" Its wings were two blurs slicing through the air and roaring like kettledrums. The ground below streamed backwards. David looked back again. The Gryffons were falling into the distance. Their cries were getting fainter. Now they looked like a flock of starlings . . . now like a cluster of flies . . . now like gnats. And then they had faded out of sight, and David and the Phoenix were streaking over the grassland alone.

Ten minutes later they reached a shore and landed. They flopped on the sand, panting. And David, suddenly feeling very faint, closed his eyes and put his head between his knees. After they had got their breath, the Phoenix patted David on the shoulder and said huskily:

"I congratulate you, my boy. Your plan was magnificent — precisely what *I* should have done, had I thought of it first. Needless to say, we shall not go on looking for the Gryffins. But now you know exactly what they are like: midway in size between the Gryffens and Gryffons, and reddish in color. Most amiable souls, willing to do anything for anyone. It is hard to believe that they are all related. But enough, my boy. Let us go home."

As soon as they reached the ledge, the Phoenix put David down and prepared to take off again.

"Where are you going, Phoenix?" David asked.

"Some business to attend to, my boy."

Muttering under its breath something that sounded like "tail feathers, indeed!" the Phoenix soared off. And David, stiff and sore and thoroughly tired, started down the mountainside for home.

5: *In Which the Scientist
Arrives in Pursuit
of the Phoenix, and
There Are Alarums and
Excursions by Night*

THE LIGHTS DOWNSTAIRS
were all on when David got home, and as soon as he
opened the front door he could tell that they had company.

He shouted, "I'm home!" and sneezed. The dust
from the Gryffons' cave still clung to him, tickling his
nose.

"Well, here he is at last," said Dad's voice. "Come

on in, David." Then, as David walked into the living room, "Good heavens, Son, what's happened to you?"

"Your *back*, David!" Mother said in a horrified voice. "Your poor back! What *happened* to you?"

David felt himself. The back of his shirt was ripped to tatters, and there were three lines of caked blood across his shoulders. He remembered now: it was the

Gryffon that had tried to grab him as he and the Phoenix made their escape. But he had promised the Phoenix to keep its secret.

He stammered, "I — I had an accident."

"And dust all *over* you!" Mother went on.

"Well," said David desperately, "it was a *dusty* accident."

"It seems to have been very dusty indeed," said a third voice. There was a loud sneeze.

David's father jumped up. "You gave me such a shock when you came in that I almost forgot, David. We have a guest." And he introduced David to a very tall, thin man with a bald head. His face and neck were burnt red by the sun, and he had on a pair of thick glasses which made his pale eyes look immense. For some reason David took an instant dislike to him, but he shook hands politely and said, "How do you do?"

"David, eh?" said the man. "Well, well. Are you a good boy, David?"

Of all the stupid questions in the world, that was the one David hated most. He clenched his teeth and looked the other way.

"David, dear," said Mother with an awkward laugh, "I think you'd better go upstairs and wash and change."

When David came into the living room again, the guest was talking excitedly. ". . . completely unknown to man," he was saying. "It's the discovery of the age. My name will be famous if I succeed in my plans."

"How fascinating!" Mother said. "And to think of it happening right here!"

"And it's huge," the guest said, "simply huge. And brilliantly colored. For a scientist like myself, it's more than fascinating."

David was listening now. Scientist? *Scientist!* His heart missed a beat, and he choked. Oh, no, it couldn't be *the* Scientist. *Or could it?*

"David here spends all his time up on the mountain," his father said. "Maybe he's seen it."

The guest turned his big, pale, unpleasant eyes on David. "Well, David," he said, "maybe you can help me. Now, have you seen anything unusual on the mountain?"

"Unusual?" said David unsteadily. There was a pain in his chest from the pounding of his heart.

"Yes, David," the guest went on, "unusual. So unusual that you couldn't miss it: a very large bird with bright plumage."

The floor under David seemed to rock. It was true, then — it was horribly true. This was the Scientist who

64

had been chasing the Phoenix. This was their enemy.

"Bird?" David dodged. "Wh-wh-why, there are lots of birds up there. Sparrows and meadow larks and — and sparrows . . ."

"But nothing like a huge bird with bright feathers?"

Well, he would have to tell a lie. After all, it was for the Phoenix's sake.

"No," said David.

"Ah," said the Scientist. But his cold eyes bored into David's for another instant, plainly saying, "I'm not fooled, young man."

"It's odd," he continued, "that no one has seen it. But I have no doubt it's somewhere here. I am going to begin my search as soon as my equipment gets here."

"Tell us about it," said Mother politely.

"Well, I discovered it on the other side of the valley, you know," said the Scientist eagerly. "Quite by accident — I was really looking for another species. Now, birds, you know, have fixed habits. If you know those habits, you can predict just what they will do at any time. This particular bird was a daytime creature, so I tried to watch it between dawn and dusk. But it seemed to have a mind of its own — you might almost say an intelligence. It avoided me in a very clever way, and it avoided my traps also. Uncanny! So after several weeks I decided to shoot it if I got the chance. Then suddenly it disappeared, but I'm certain it came over to this side of the valley — "

There was no escape from the subject during dinner. The Scientist could think and talk of nothing else. He described the merits of deadfalls, snares, steel traps, and birdlime. He asked which they thought would make the best bait, a rabbit, a beefsteak, a live lamb, or carrion. He told them all about the new high-powered, long-range rifle which he had ordered. And he vowed to them all that he would not rest until the bird was either caught or killed "for the advancement of human learning."

David listened with horror. The dinner before him went untouched. His only thought was that now he would have to warn the Phoenix as soon as possible. The Phoenix would go to South America after all, and his education would end before it had even started. All because of this hateful man! He fought to hold back his tears.

Dinner was over at last. David mumbled his excuses and ducked out of the dining room, but Aunt Amy seized him firmly just as he thought he had got away.

"Bedtime for you, David," she said firmly.

"Oh, Aunt Amy, please! I've got to — "

"Upstairs, young man. You've had enough galli-vanting around for one day. You're all worn out."

"I'm *not!*" said David, struggling. "I feel fine. Look, I just *have* to — "

It was useless. She marched him upstairs to his room and stood in the doorway until he had undressed and put on his pajamas and got into bed.

"Now," she said, "you go to sleep. The mountain will still be there in the morning — unless there's a land-slide. Good night." And she turned out the light and shut the door.

This was awful! He could not sneak downstairs, be-cause the stairs could be seen from the living room. He could not climb out of his window, because a rose arbor was directly beneath it, and he would be ripped by the thorns. And Mother always came in to say good night before she went to bed. If he was not there when she came in tonight, there would be a lot of unpleasant ex-plaining to do. The only thing, then, was to wait until the Scientist went home and everyone was in bed.

It was a maddening wait. The Scientist's voice went on and on like the drone of an electric fan, interrupted only by an occasional murmur from Mother or Dad. For a while David sat in bed twisting the sheets in his hands;

then he got up and paced the room in his bare feet. It seemed to him that three or four whole nighttimes had passed before he finally heard all three voices raised and talking at once.

The Scientist was going! Now they were saying good-by at the front door . . . now the door was being closed . . . now there were footsteps on the stairs. He jumped into bed just before Mother put her head in and said, "Good night, dear." David murmured, pretending to be half asleep. His door closed again. The light switches snapped, and there was silence.

He waited another half hour to make sure everyone was asleep. As quickly and silently as he could, he pulled on his clothes, crept out of his room, and slid cautiously down the bannister. In the back yard he put on his shoes, dived through the hedge, and started to race up the mountainside.

Fortunately there was a nearly-full moon and no clouds in the sky. But even with this light, it was not easy to keep to the trail. Several times he lost his way, so that the trip took much longer than usual. But he found the ledge at last, climbed over the final difficult rock, and sat down to catch his breath. When he could speak, he called softly:

"Phoenix!"

There was no answer.

"Phoenix!" He pushed through the thicket to the other side of the ledge. *"Phoenix!"*

The Phoenix was gone.

The tears that had been stopped up all evening could be held no longer. David dropped to the ground, leaned his forehead against a rock, and let them go. He had just remembered. As soon as they had come back from the Gryffon adventure, the Phoenix had flown off on some sort of business. And it had not said when it would return.

The tears cleared David's mind and made him feel better. Now what? He began to think. If he stayed on the ledge all night, they might find out at home and make a terrible fuss. But if he did not warn the Phoenix before morning, the Scientist might creep up while the bird was resting and trap it or shoot it. So he would have to warn the Phoenix *and* return home. And the only way to do both these things was to write the Phoenix a note.

But he had neither paper nor pencil.

A fine mess he had made of everything! Now he would have to go all the way back home, write the note, come all the way back up to the ledge, and then go home again.

DAVID AND THE PHOENIX

David trudged down the mountainside in a very low mood. Now that he had a definite plan to work on, his fear was gone, but he felt that he had been pretty stupid to rush off without thinking of everything first. In his mind he could hear the Phoenix saying, "Look before you leap, my boy," and other wise words of advice. And he had cried, too. Lucky that no one had been there to see *that*.

As he approached the house he was surprised to see all the lights ablaze and to hear his name being called. "Oh-oh," he thought, "they've found out I've gone."

"Here I am!" he shouted, opening the door. "What's the matter?"

It was a strange sight which met him inside. Dad, in his gay pajamas, was waving a revolver and making fierce noises. Mother, looking frightened, had a shoe in one hand. Aunt Amy, with her hair in rags, was also well-armed — with a big cast-iron frying pan. Beckie was howling upstairs.

"David!" Mother cried. "Are you all right? Where have you been? Did he hurt you?"

"Who?" said David. "I'm all right. What's the matter?"

"The burglar!" said Mother excitedly. "He put his head in the window and said '*psssst!*'"

"I tell you, burglars don't say *psssst!*" Dad said. "They try to make as little noise as possible. Just let me catch him doing it again!" he added, waving his pistol.

"Running around on that mountain at all hours of the night," Aunt Amy grumbled, "with burglars and I don't know what-all loose in town!"

"And then we found that you were gone, and we thought he had stolen you," Mother went on. "Where have you been?"

"I couldn't sleep," said David. "So I went for a walk."

"Well, thank heavens you're safe," said Mother.

"Hankering after that mountain all night," Aunt Amy muttered. "As if he wasn't up there all day."

"Look here, Son," said Dad. "What do you know about this?"

"Honestly, Dad," said David, "I couldn't sleep. There's nothing wrong with that. I can't help it if I can't sleep. So I took a walk. There's nothing wrong with — "

"Oh, all right, all right," his father said. "I suppose it's just a coincidence. Let's all get back to sleep. And, David, the next time you can't sleep, try counting sheep."

Gradually the house calmed down. Beckie stopped wailing, Dad put away his gun, good nights were said, the lights were turned off.

David knew that it would be at least an hour before he dared to move again, and he would have to be doubly careful this time. And he was a little nervous himself now about that burglar. What if he should meet him when he went out again? He tried to forget about that by thinking of what he would put in the note for the Phoenix.

He had got as far as "Dear Phoenix:" and was wondering how you spelled "Phoenix," when there came a swish and a thump at his window, followed by a cautious whisper:

"*Psssst!*"

David felt his scalp prickle. "Wh-wh-who's that?" he quavered.

"Is that you, my boy?" whispered a familiar, guarded voice. "Ah, thank heavens!"

And the Phoenix crawled through the window.

Weak with relief, David snapped on the bedside light. The Phoenix presented a shocking sight. Its face was drawn with fatigue, and it looked rather draggled. Its back sagged, its wings drooped to the floor, and it walked with a limp.

"Oh, Phoenix, Phoenix!" David whispered. He jumped to support the bird before it collapsed entirely.

"Ah, thank you, my boy," the Phoenix murmured. "Your bed, I presume? May I? Thank you." The springs creaked under its weight as the Phoenix gingerly lay down.

"What a night, my boy, *what* a night!" it sighed weakly, closing its eyes.

"Oh, Phoenix, what happened? Can I do anything for you?" David whispered.

"A damp, cooling cloth upon my forehead would be welcome, my boy," murmured the Phoenix. "Also a bit of nourishment."

David slid down the bannister, got a handful of cookies and a glass of milk, and dampened a dish towel. When he returned, the Phoenix was fast asleep.

"Phoenix," he whispered, "wake up. Here's your — "

The Phoenix awoke with a violent start and stared wildly around the room. "Trapped!" it muttered, making a frenzied effort to get off the bed.

"Not so *loud!*" David whispered sharply. "It's me!"

Understanding dawned in the Phoenix's eyes, and it eased itself back with a sigh. "Ah, you, my boy. You gave me quite a fright. I thought — " But here the Phoenix caught sight of the milk and cookies and sat up again.

"Ambrosia," it sighed reverently. "And nectar. You *are* a prince, my dear fellow!" And the Phoenix reached out eagerly.

"Now, Phoenix," David whispered as he wrapped the wet towel around the Phoenix's head, "what's happened?"

"Ah, that feels heavenly, my boy! (Munch munch.) What has happened? (Munch munch. Gulp.) I was insulted, I accepted a challenge, and I brilliantly maintained my honor. Let that be a lesson to you, my boy: death before dishonor. Yes, in spite of my age, I — "

"But Phoenix, what *happened?*"

"To be brief, then, my boy, for brevity is the soul of wit — although I am not trying to be witty now; I am simply too worn out — Brevity — ah — where was I?"

"I *think* you were telling me what happened to you tonight," David said.

"Ah, yes, quite so! Well, I raced the Witch, to put it quite simply."

"Oh, Phoenix! Did you win?"

"She said that she would 'beat my tail feathers off,' did she not? Behold, my dear fellow — every tail feather intact!"

"Good for you, Phoenix! How did it go?"

"I found her somewhere over Scotland and accepted her challenge. We jockeyed about for starting positions, and she insulted me by offering me a handicap — which, of course, I refused. For several hundred miles it was nip and tuck, as it were. Then, over Luxembourg, I put all my energies into a magnificent sprint and won the race by three and a half broom lengths. She claimed a foul and went off in a fit of sulks, of course. (I never saw a Witch who was a good loser.) And I — well, the fact is, my boy, that I am not as young as I used to be. I simply *crawled* home."

"Oh, you poor Phoenix! But you won, though.

Good for you, Phoenix. I'm proud of you! I didn't like her at all."

"There you are — I had to win, for both of us. Now, as I wended my weary way homeward, I realized that I would be too tired to go traveling tomorrow. So I decided to tell you, in case you should want to do something else during the day. But I did not know which house was yours. I had to pick one at random. I thrust my head in a window and uttered a cautious *psssssst!* Imagine my dismay when I was answered by a piercing scream! I had to beat a hasty and undignified retreat into a garage until all was peaceful again. Then I did the same thing at the next house, and the next, with the same results." The Phoenix sighed. "Would you believe it, my boy? — this is the fifth house I tried. But I knew I was on the right track when I heard them calling for you."

"Oh, so it was *you*," said David. "You almost frightened Mother to death. She thought you were a burglar."

"My dear fellow, I am really sorry for having caused any misunderstanding or fright," said the Phoenix apologetically. "It was just that I wanted to tell you of my victory — that is, to tell you that I should be indisposed tomorrow."

Then David recalled that he had something to say

too. The shock of remembering was such that he blurted out the news without thinking of softening the blow.

"Phoenix, listen! The Scientist is here!"

The Phoenix sat up in bed with a jerk, and David barely suppressed its startled exclamation by clamping a hand over its beak.

"It's not so bad yet," he whispered hurriedly, "because he's not sure where you are, and he has to wait for his equipment to get here. But, oh, Phoenix, now I suppose you'll go to South America after all, and I won't have any more education."

The Phoenix leaped to its feet and struck a defiant pose. "My boy," it said angrily, "you are mistaken. I refuse to be chased around any longer. Even the lowly worm turns. Am I a mouse, or am I the Phoenix? If that insufferable man wishes to pursue me further, if he cannot mind his own business, then, by Jove, we shall meet him face to face and FIGHT TO THE FINISH!"

Its voice, which had been getting louder and louder, ended in an indignant squawk (its battle cry, as it explained later). David's warning ssh! was too late. They heard rapid footsteps and the sound of light switches snapping.

"Quick!" David said. "Out the window!"

With a hasty "Farewell, my boy," the Phoenix plunged headlong toward the window — and tripped over the sill. There was a resounding crash outside as the bird landed on the rose arbor, a brief but furious thrashing and muttering, and then the receding flurry of wings.

Dad burst into the room with his revolver, followed by Mother and Aunt Amy (with two frying pans, this time).

"He stuck his head in the window and said *psssst!* at me!" David cried. "A big dark shape in the window!"

This time Dad telephoned the police. In no time at all, three carloads of weary policemen were swarming over the house and yard, with guns and flashlights drawn. It was the fifth — or was it the sixth? — call they had received from the neighborhood that night, they explained. There followed an hour of questions, arguments, and theories, during which everyone became very excited. Everyone, that is, except David — although he acted excited to avoid suspicion. But he was happy. He had warned the Phoenix, the Phoenix was going to stay, and there was nothing to worry about until tomorrow.

6: *In Which the Phoenix Has a Plan, and David and the Phoenix Call On a Sea Monster*

"WELL, YOU'RE IN ALL THE papers this morning, Phoenix," said David, as he sat down beside the reclining bird next morning. "They don't know who you are, but they're all talking about what happened last night. They call you the 'Whispering Burglar.' The police are pretty worried."

"My dear chap," said the Phoenix apologetically,

79

"let me repeat my sincere regrets for causing alarm. It was not my desire to — the *police,* did you say? Have they discovered any clues?"

"No," said David reassuringly. "They can't find a thing. They think the Whispering Burglar climbed up a ladder to say *pssssst!* into the upstairs windows. Only they can't find the ladder. They call it the 'Missing Mystery Clue.' "

The Phoenix gazed at the sky and mused. "In all the papers, you say? Well, Fame at last — although hardly the kind I had expected. What a pity that there can be no photographs with the story. Imagine a picture of me on the front page! A profile, perhaps — or would a full-length shot be more effective? Or both, let us say, with — "

"I know you'd look very handsome, Phoenix," David interrupted, "but what we *should* be thinking about is the Scientist. What are we going to do?"

"Oh, *that,*" said the Phoenix. "I was coming to that, my boy. The battle is already half won. I have a Plan."

"Good for you, Phoenix! What is it?"

"Aha!" said the Phoenix, with a mysterious smile. "All will unfold in time. Rest assured that the Plan is brilliant. In one stroke of genius it solves everything.

Tactics, my boy! Napoleon had nothing on me."

"But what *is* it, Phoenix?"

"Tut, my boy," said the Phoenix in a maddening way. "Control your impatience. You will see. Now, we shall have to buy some things, so we shall need money. Let me see . . . Several of the Leprechauns have large pots of gold . . . No, I fear they would not part with so much as a penny. Tightfisted, my dear fellow! — you never saw such misers. Hmmm . . . Well, there are the Dragons, of course; they guard heaps of treasure in caves. But no — they are excellent chaps in most respects, but frightfully stuffy about loans and gifts. No . . . The Djinn? No, his money is all tied up in Arabian oil specula- tion. Aha! Why didn't I think of that before? The Sea Monster, of course!"

"Do Sea Monsters have money?" asked David.

"No, but the Sea Monster should know where pirate treasure is buried — quite in its nautical line. We shall visit the Monster, my boy. Tomorrow, of course — I could not fly a foot today to save my life. My muscles are killing me!"

"Oh, poor Phoenix!" David said. But he was so ex- cited that he could not feel much pity. Pirate treasure! They were going to dig for pirate treasure!

"We shall need a spade. I trust you will arrange for it, my boy?"

"Of course, Phoenix," said David, jumping to his feet. "I'll get everything ready right away. Don't move till I get back."

"Impossible, my boy." The Phoenix groaned as it shifted into a more comfortable position.

David raced home to collect the necessary things for the trip. Remembering how cold it had been last time, he took his leather jacket out of the closet, and a pair of gloves and a scarf. For the Phoenix he borrowed a bottle of liniment and took all the cookies from the cooky jar. And he picked the shortest of three spades in the garage. During the rest of the day he massaged the Phoenix's back and wings with the liniment. He was exploding with curiosity about the Plan, of course. But the Phoenix would only smile its smuggest smile and tell him to "wait and see, wait and see" — which almost drove David mad.

Tomorrow took its time, the way it always does when you are anxious to see it arrive, but it finally came. And David found himself with the spade held tightly under one arm, his jacket zipped up to his chin, gloves on, and scarf knotted, all ready to go.

"To the west, this time," said the Phoenix, as David got up on its back. "This is the Monster's Pacific season, you know. Ready, my boy? Splendid! We are off!"

Over the mountains and desert they sped, over the shore, out across the ocean. For a long time they hurtled through a huge blue loneliness, dark blue below, lighter blue above. Once they passed over a ship, a pencil dot trailing a pin-scratch of white. Another time they startled a high-flying albatross, which gave a frightened squawk and plunged down out of sight with folded wings. Aside from that, there was nothing to see until they reached the islands.

The Phoenix slowed down to a glide and dropped lower. "These are the coral atolls of the Pacific, my boy," it called over its shoulder. "That lake in the center of each island is called the lagoon."

David was enchanted by the atolls. They were made of tiny islets, strung together like the beads of a necklace. And the colors! The dark blue of the sea became lighter around the islands, melting from sapphire to turquoise to jade. The atolls were ringed with dazzling white surf and beach, and they all had cool green swaths of palm trees and underbrush. And each lagoon also had its varying shades of blue, like the outer sea.

"I fear we may have trouble, my boy," said the Phoenix, as they scanned the empty beaches. "The Monster shifts about from island to island to avoid discovery. We shall just have to search."

And search they did, atoll after atoll, until at the end of an hour they were rewarded. David suddenly spotted a dark object stretched out on the beach of a lagoon, and at the same time the Phoenix said "Aha!" triumphantly. They began to spiral down.

The Sea Monster was immense. Its body could have filled the living room at home. Its neck was twenty feet long, and so was its tail (which ended in a barbed point). It had huge seal-like flippers, and its polished brown hide was made up of scales as big as dinner plates.

"Wake up, Monster!" The Phoenix cried. "We — "

The next instant they were lost in a cloud of flying sand and spray, through which could be heard a prodigious splash. When it had cleared, they found themselves alone on the beach. The only sign of the Sea Monster was a great furrow in the sand, which led down to the agitated water.

"Golly, that was fast!" David marveled, as they shook the sand from themselves. "Do you think it'll come back, Phoenix?"

"Of course, my boy. Curiosity, if nothing else, will bring it up again. In the meantime, we might as well sit down and wait."

They sat down and waited. David took off his jacket. For fifteen minutes they heard nothing but the murmuring of the surf and the rustling clatter of palm fronds. At last there was a slight splashing noise from the lagoon.

"There," David whispered, pointing.

Thirty feet offshore, an ear was being thrust cautiously above the rippled surface. It twitched once or twice, then pointed quiveringly in their direction.

"Come out, Monster!" the Phoenix shouted. "It is I, the Phoenix."

The Sea Monster's head appeared slowly, followed by several yards of neck. It peered at them short-sightedly, weaving its head from side to side to get a better view. David saw that it had two short, straight horns just in front of its ears, eyes that were soft and cowlike, and a most expressive set of whiskers. The whiskers were now at a doubtful, half-mast angle.

"Ah, Phoenix," said the Sea Monster at last in a mild voice. "Can't you remember to wake me a bit more gently? I thought you were — "

"Come on out," said the Phoenix firmly, "and stop looking like a lost sheep."

"Uh — what about — uh — that?" said the Sea Monster hesitantly, pointing one ear at David.

"This," said the Phoenix, "is David. He is getting an education. I assure you that he will not bite."

The Sea Monster swam toward them, heaved itself out of the water, and offered its huge flipper for David to shake.

"Sorry I rushed off like that," it said. "The trouble is, I've had such a bad case of war nerves. Why, sometimes I jump out of my skin at nothing at all."

"Were you in the war?" David asked.

"Ah, *was* I," sighed the Sea Monster. It flopped down comfortably on its belly, curled its tail around its front flippers, and sighed again. But David noticed that its whiskers had perked up to a quite cheerful angle. The Sea Monster was obviously delighted to have someone listen to its troubles.

"Yes," it said, heaving a third sigh, "I was. From the very beginning, much against my will. Guns all over the place! Terrible!"

"Did they shoot you?" David asked, horrified.

"Well, *at* me, anyway. I'm thankful to say they never hit me, but there were some pretty near misses. All the oceans were simply packed with ships. I couldn't lift my head out of water without bringing down a perfect rain of shells and bullets."

"The *intelligent* thing in that case," the Phoenix broke in with a sniff, "would have been to stay *under* water."

"Thank you, Phoenix," said the Sea Monster dryly. "But I *do* like to breathe now and then. Anyway, I wasn't safe even under water. They'd drop depth charges on me. One ship even launched a torpedo at me!"

"How awful!" said David.

"Tut! my boy," said the Phoenix. "I have no doubt our friend is stretching the truth shamelessly. You need not look so smug, Monster. You were not the only one in the war. *I* have gone through anti-aircraft fire a number of times. Some of it was very severe. In fact, once I — "

"Once I had the whole North Atlantic fleet after *me,*" the Sea Monster interrupted proudly.

"And *I* remember the Franco-Prussian War!" said the Phoenix. "Which, I daresay, you do *not.*"

"Well — uh — no, I don't."

"There you are!" the Phoenix crowed.

The Sea Monster, looking rather ruffled, pointedly turned from the Phoenix and said to David, "What would you like to do, David?"

David suddenly remembered what they had come for, and the excitement rushed back into his heart. He opened his mouth to cry "We want to dig for treasure!" and then stopped short. Asking for money, he knew, was an impolite thing to do — especially from someone you had only just met. And there was no telling how the Sea

Monster might feel about people nosing around for its treasure. So he looked at the Phoenix and waited for it to speak.

The Phoenix caught David's glance, cleared its throat several times, and looked apologetically at the Sea Monster. "Monster, old chap," it said soothingly, "I am deeply sorry for having doubted you just now. Deeply sorry."

"Quite all right," said the Sea Monster stiffly.

"Yes," the Phoenix continued, "we both know that you have passed through perilous times, through dangers which (I must confess) would have left *me* a shattered wreck."

The Sea Monster sighed sadly, but its whiskers were beginning to rise again.

"The Monster bears up very well under this fearful strain — don't you think so, my boy? A splendid example for the rest of us. Magnificent."

The Sea Monster's whiskers were quivering with pleasure.

"Monster, old chap, old friend, you were never one to let a boon companion down. If I have said it once, I have said it a hundred times: 'The Sea Monster,' I have said, 'the Sea Monster is the helpful sort. Mention the words Staunch Friend,' I have said, 'and immediately the Sea Monster comes to mind.' "

The Phoenix reached up one wing and began to pat the Sea Monster's flipper.

"Monster, old chum, we — ah — we — Well, the plain fact is that we — ah — we have need of — such a trifling matter" (here the Phoenix gave a careless laugh) "that I should not really bring it up at all. Ah — we need a bit of money."

"Oh," said the Sea Monster. Its whiskers sagged.

"Now, please do not be offended, Monster," said the Phoenix hastily. "After all, you have no need for the treasure, and it does absolutely no good buried under the ground."

"It doesn't do any harm there, either," said the Sea Monster. "Really, Phoenix, I never thought *you* — "

"Monster," said the Phoenix solemnly, *"this* — is a matter of life or death."

"Life or death — ha!"

"Please, Monster," said David. "It really is life or death, because the Scientist is chasing the Phoenix, and the Phoenix has a plan to escape him, and we need some money to carry out the plan so the Scientist can't hurt the Phoenix."

"A few small coins will do," added the Phoenix, with a winning smile. "A louis d'or, for example, or some pieces of eight. After which you may bury the rest again."

"*Please*, Monster!" David begged.

The Monster looked at David, and at the Phoenix, and then at David again, and then at the lagoon. It sighed a very doubtful sigh.

"Oh . . . all right," it said reluctantly. "But for goodness sake, don't go telling anyone where you found it."

"Of course not," said the Phoenix. And David leaped up and shouted "Hooray!" and grabbed the spade and his jacket.

"The stuff is on the next island," said the Sea Monster. "I can swim over with you two on my back. This way, please — we have to leave from the outer beach."

The Sea Monster was a magnificent swimmer. Its neck cut through the water like the stem of a Viking ship, and it left a frothing wake behind. Every once in a while it would plunge its head into the water and come up with a fish, which it would swallow whole.

"Would you like some breakfast, David?" said the Sea Monster.

"No, thank you," David answered, "but you go right ahead. Phoenix," he added, "what *are* you doing?"

The Phoenix, which had been walking up and down with its wings clasped behind its back, stopped and gazed over the sea. "Pacing the quarter-deck, my boy. Scanning the horizon. That is what one usually does at sea, I believe."

"You'll be wanting us to call you Admiral next," said the Sea Monster acidly.

They steamed on. Twenty minutes and seventy-six large breakfast fish later they sighted the island — a little smudge on the horizon, dead ahead.

"Land ho!" a voice croaked. "Thank heavens."

David turned in surprise. The Phoenix was no longer pacing the quarter-deck and scanning the horizon.

It was sitting limply with its head down and a glassy stare in its eyes.

"You had better hurry up," David said to the Sea Monster. "I think the Phoenix is seasick."

"Am not," the Phoenix gasped. "Merely (ulp!) temporary."

The Sea Monster turned and smiled sweetly at the Phoenix. "You'll get used to it in no time, Admiral."

When they landed, however, the Phoenix recovered rapidly and even began to put on a slight nautical swagger. The Sea Monster humped off down the beach, followed eagerly by the two treasure hunters. In a few minutes it came to a halt and sniffed the sand very carefully, swinging its head snakelike to and fro. It settled on one spot, sniffed it thoroughly, felt the sand with its whiskers, and then solemnly announced: "Here."

"Ahoy, me hearties!" the Phoenix shouted. "Turn to and stand by to splice the main brace! Steady as she goes, mates!"

David needed no encouragement from anyone. He began to dig furiously. Flashing in the sun, the spade bit into the beach, and coarse white sand spurted in all directions. The Phoenix was quite as excited as David. It danced around the deepening hole with eyes asparkle, shouting such piratical terms as "Shiver me timbers!" "Strike your colors!" and "Give 'em no quarter, lads!" Suddenly it began to beat time with its wing and to sing in a raucous voice:

> "Cut the King's throat and take the King's gold —
> Heave ho, bullies, for Panama!
> There's plenty of loot for the lad who is bold —
> Heave away, bullies, for Panama!"

"You're flat on that last note," said the Sea Monster.

"My dear Monster, I have perfect pitch!"

"Oh, yes — you have perfect sea legs, too."

"Well, ah — How are you coming along, my boy? Any signs of treasure?"

David did not hear. In fact he heard nothing from

the first crunch of the spade onward. His education was now richer by this fact: once you start out after treasure, you can think of nothing else until it is found. The sun was beating hotly on him, little rivulets of sweat poured down his face and arms, his muscles ached, blisters were beginning to form on his hands. Heedless of all, he dug on. He had settled into the rhythm of it now, and nothing could distract him.

"Tell you what's a good thing for seasickness," said the Sea Monster slyly. "You take a — " Pretending not to hear, the Phoenix stood first on one leg and then on the other and stared into the sky. David dug tirelessly.

Suddenly the spade grated on something solid, and they all jumped. David shouted "Here it is!" and shoveled up sand frantically. The Phoenix danced around the hole, also shouting. Even the Sea Monster arched its neck to get a better view. They could see a brass ring, crusted with verdigris, fastened to a partly-exposed piece of wood. The sand flew. Now they could see studded strips of metal bound to the wood, and a rusty padlock. And in a few minutes a whole chest, with slanting sides and a curved lid and tarnished brass hinges, was uncovered. David threw the spade on the beach, seized the brass handle, and tugged. It came off in his hand.

"Here, let me," said the Sea Monster. David got out of the hole, and the Sea Monster worked one flipper carefully under the chest. "Look out," it said, and heaved its flipper up. The chest shot into the air, tumbled down end over end, and split wide open on the beach.

David gasped. A dazzling, sparkling heap spilled out on the sand. There were heaps of gold and silver coins, the silver black with tarnish but the gold still bright. There were pearls, rubies, diamonds, beryls, emeralds, opals, sapphires, amethysts. And bracelets, necklaces, pendants, sunbursts, brooches, rings, pins, combs, buckles, lockets, buttons, crucifixes. And carved pieces of jade and ivory and coral and jet. And coronets, crowns, tiaras, arm bands. And jeweled daggers, picture frames, vases, silver knives and forks and spoons, sugar bowls, platters, goblets.

For an hour they examined the treasure. David fairly wallowed in it, exclaiming "Look at this one!" or "Oh, how beautiful!" or just "Golly!" The Phoenix muttered such things as "King's ransom" and "Wealth of the Indies." The Sea Monster was not interested in the treasure, but kept glancing nervously out to sea.

At last the Phoenix said, "Well, my boy, I think we had better make our choice. Three or four coins should do it."

The Sea Monster gave a relieved sigh. "Let's get the rest of it underground right away. You have no idea what trouble it can cause."

The choice was difficult. There were so many coins, all of them with queer writing and heads of unknown gods and kings. David finally picked out four gold pieces and tied them up in his handkerchief. Then the Sea Monster swept the rest of the treasure into the hole. They all pushed sand in on top of it and jumped on the mound till it was level with the rest of the beach.

The Phoenix turned to the Sea Monster and said solemnly: "Monster, old fellow, I knew you would not fail us. You stood forth in our hour of need, and we shall not forget."

And David echoed, "Thank you, Monster."

The Sea Monster ducked its head and blushed. A wave of fiery red started at its nose, traveled rapidly back over its ears, down its neck, along the body, and fanned out to the tips of its flippers and the extreme end of the barb in its tail.

Even its whiskers turned pink.

"Well — uh — glad.to help — uh — nothing to it, really," it mumbled. Then it turned abruptly, galloped down to the sea, plunged into the surf, and was gone.

7: *In Which the Phoenix's*
Plan Is Carried Out, and
There Are More Alarums
and Excursions in the Night

"NOW, MY BOY," SAID THE
Phoenix, when they got back to the ledge that afternoon,
"are the shops still open?"

"I think they're open till six," said David, shaking
the sand out of his shoes. "Are we going to buy something?"

"Precisely, my boy. A hardware store should have

99

what we need. Now, you will take our gold and purchase the following." And the Phoenix listed the things it wanted, and told David which to bring to the ledge and which to leave below.

". . . and a hatchet," the Phoenix concluded.

"We have one at home already," said David. "Now, listen, Phoenix, *can't* you tell me what all this is for? What are we going to do with it?"

"My boy, the feline's existence was terminated as a direct result of its inquisitiveness."

"What did you say?"

"Curiosity killed the cat," explained the Phoenix.

"Oh. But — "

"Now, run along, my boy. A very important Thought has just come to me. I must Meditate a while." The Phoenix glanced at the thicket and hid a yawn behind one wing.

"Oh, all *right,*" said David. "I'll see you in the morning, then."

It wasn't until he got home that he thought of something. He couldn't spend pirate gold pieces, or even show them to anyone, without being asked a lot of embarrassing questions. What to do? Ask Dad or Mother or Aunt Amy to lend him some money? More embarrassing questions . . . Well, he would have to rob his bank. But wait — why hadn't he remembered? Just before they had moved, Uncle Charles had given him a ten-dollar bill as a farewell present. He had been saving it for a model airplane, but the excitement of the last few days had driven it completely out of his mind. Of course the Phoenix's Plan was more important than any model plane could be.

So he kept the gold pieces tied up in his handkerchief and took his ten dollars to a hardware store, where he bought what the Phoenix wanted — a coil of rope, an electric door bell, a pushbutton, and one hundred feet of insulated wire. Then he brought the package home, hid it behind the woodpile in the garage, and sat down to think. Wire — bell — pushbutton. What could the Phoenix possibly want with them? And what was the rope for? And the hatchet? The more he puzzled over it the more confused he became, and finally he just gave up. There was only one thing he was sure about: whatever the Plan was, they would have to carry it out as soon as possible. Two days had passed since the Scientist had shown up. The new gun he had ordered might arrive at any time now. Perhaps even today, when they had been digging up the pirate treasure, the Scientist had got his new rifle and had started to hunt through the mountains.

The thought gave David a creepy feeling on the back of his neck. They certainly would have to hurry.

Early next morning David climbed up to the ledge, bringing with him the coil of rope and the hatchet. As an afterthought he had added a paper bag full of cookies.

"Here's the stuff, Phoenix," he called out as he stepped onto the ledge. "Where are you?"

There was a crash from the thicket as though someone had jumped up in it suddenly, and the Phoenix stumbled out, rubbing its eyes.

"Ah, splendid, my boy! Yes. I was just — ah — Thinking."

"Phoenix," said David, "I'm not going to ask you again what your Plan is, because I know you'll tell me when it's time. But whatever it is, we'd better do it right now. The Scientist may show up any minute."

"Precisely, my boy. Never put off until tomorrow what can be done today. One of my favorite proverbs. We shall begin immediately — " Here the Phoenix caught sight of the bag in David's hand and added hastily: "But, of course, we must not forget that first things come first."

"You might have brought more," said the Phoenix, fifteen minutes later.

"There weren't any more in the jar," David said. "Phoenix, please tell me what we're going to do. I don't care if curiosity *did* kill the cat. I've been thinking about the rope and wire and bell all night, and I can't make heads or tails out of it."

The Phoenix gave a pleased laugh. "Of course you cannot, my boy. The Plan is far too profound for you to guess what it is. But set your mind at rest. I shall now explain the rope and hatchet."

David leaned forward eagerly.

"Now, scientists, you know, have fixed habits. If you know those habits, you can predict just what they will do at any time. Our particular Scientist is a daytime creature — that is to say, he comes at dawn and goes at dusk. His invariable habit, my boy!"

"Well?"

"There you are, my boy!" said the Phoenix triumphantly. *"We shall sleep during the day and continue your education at night!"*

"Oh," said David. He thought about this a while, then asked, "But suppose the Scientist comes up on the ledge during the day and catches you asleep?"

"Aha! That is where the rope and hatchet come in. Never fear, my boy — I thought of that also. We are going to construct a snare at each end of the ledge."

"How?"

"Hand me that twig, my boy." The Phoenix took the twig, found a bare spot of earth, and sketched a picture. "First we find a sapling and clear the branches from it with the hatchet — like this. Next we get a stake, cut a notch in it, and drive it into the ground — so. The sapling is bent down to it and fitted into the notch, which holds it down. You see, my boy? Now we make a noose — so — from a piece of rope, tie it to the end of the sapling, and spread the loop out on the path — this way. The whole snare is hidden under grass and leaves." The Phoenix beamed and flung out its wings in a dramatic gesture. "Just picture it, my dear chap! The Scientist, smiling evilly as he skulks along the path! The unwary footstep! The sapling, jarred out of the notch, springing upward! The tightened noose! And our archenemy dangling by the foot in mid-air, completely at our mercy! Magnificent!"

"Golly, Phoenix," said David, "that's pretty clever."

"*Clever,* my boy? Better to say 'a stroke of genius.' Only I, Phoenix, could have thought of it. And consider the poetic justice of it! This is exactly the sort of trap that the Scientist once set for me! Well, shall we begin?"

The Phoenix had made the snares sound delightfully simple, but they soon discovered that the job was harder than it sounded. First they had to find the right kind of sapling, springy and strong. The sapling had to be in the right place — one by the goat trail, the other at the far

end of the ledge. When they had been chosen, David had to shinny up them to lop off their branches. That was a very awkward business; the saplings swayed and trembled under his weight, and he could only use one hand for the hatchet. Then he had to make two stakes from stout, hard wood, cut a notch at one end, and drive them into the ground with the flat of the hatchet. But the hardest part was trying to bend the sapling down to the stake and fitting it into the notch. It took the weight of both of them to bring the sapling to the ground. If they got the slightest bit off balance, it would spring up again. Once David fell off; the sapling went *swish!* back into the air, flinging the astonished Phoenix thirty feet up the mountainside.

It was not until afternoon, when the sun had turned ruddy and shadows were beginning to stretch dark fingers across the land, that they finished the job. But at last the saplings were set in the notches, the nooses were formed and fastened on. Grass and leaves were strewn over the snares; chips, hewn branches, and other evidences of their work were removed. They sat down and looked proudly at each other.

"My boy," said the Phoenix, "I have had a wide, and sometimes painful, experience with traps; so you may believe me when I say that these are among the best I have seen. We have done well."

"They're sure strong enough," David agreed, flexing his fingers to take the stiffness out of them. "But what are we going to do if the Scientist does get caught in one?"

"We shall burn that bridge when we reach it, my boy. Now, do you have the pliers, wire-cutters, and screw driver below?"

"Yes, they're down in the cellar. What are we going to do with them, Phoenix?"

"Patience, patience! You will be told when the time comes. I shall meet you tonight after dark, as soon as it is safe for me to come down. I trust you will have everything ready?"

"Are you coming *down?*"

"Precisely, my boy. A risk, I admit, but a necessary one. There is a hedge at the back of your house, is there not? Splendid. You may await me there."

David, sitting in the shadow of the hedge, jumped when he heard the Phoenix's quiet "Good evening, my boy."

"Phoenix," he whispered, "how did you do it? Golly, I didn't see you at all, and it isn't even dark yet."

"I have been hunted long enough, my boy, to have learned a few tricks. It is merely a matter of gliding close to the ground, selecting the best shadows, and keeping a sharp lookout. Well, let us get on with the Plan. Have you the tools here?"

"Yes, here they are."

"Splendid! Now, my boy, since we must continue your education during the night, it is necessary that we have some way of getting in touch with each other. If you climb the mountainside in the dark, you may unwittingly fall into our own snare. It is far easier for me to come down than it is for you to go up, and under cover of darkness I can do it quite safely. The question now is, how will you know when I have arrived? That, my boy, is the nub, or crux, of the situation. A difficult problem, you will admit. But I have worked out the solution."

The Phoenix lowered its voice impressively.

"My boy, we are going to install this bell in your room, and the pushbutton on the base of that telephone pole. When I arrive here at night, I shall press the button to let you know that I am ready to go. A magnificent idea, isn't it?"

It did not seem very practical to David. "Well, Phoenix, that's a good idea," he said carefully. "But how are we going to hide the wires? And what about the noise of the bell?"

"Nothing to it, my boy! The wires? There are wires between your house and the telephone pole already — one more would not be noticed. The noise? You have a pillow on your bed, under which the bell can be muffled."

"Yes, that's true." It still sounded impractical.

"Just imagine it!" the Phoenix continued enthusiastically. "Perhaps later we can install another bell at this end. Then we could learn Morse code and send messages to each other. Exactly like a private telephone line!"

Put in this way, the idea had a certain appeal, and David found himself warming to it. But there was another thing to consider.

"How about electricity, Phoenix?"

"Look above you, my boy! The telephone pole is simply loaded down with power lines waiting to be tapped."

The Phoenix was evidently set on carrying out the Plan, and David did not want to wear out the bird's patience with more objections. And — well, why not? There should be no harm in trying it out, anyway.

They gathered up the tools and walked along the hedge to the telephone pole, which was in one corner of the yard. The Phoenix began to uncoil the wire, while David gazed up doubtfully at the shadowy maze of lines and insulators on the cross-arms.

"Electricity," said the Phoenix thoughtfully, "is a complicated and profound subject. There are amperes, and there are volts, and there are kilowatt hours. I might also mention positive and negative and — ah — all that sort of thing. Most profound. Perhaps I had better investigate up there. Screw driver, please."

The Phoenix took the screw driver in one claw and flew up to the top of the pole. David could hear the creak of the lines under the Phoenix's weight and the rattling of the screw driver against the porcelain insulators. For some minutes the Phoenix investigated, clicking and scraping about, and muttering "Quite so" and "There we are." Then it fluttered down again and rubbed its wings together.

"The whole situation up there is a lot simpler than I thought it would be, my boy. The power lines merely come up to the pole on one side, pass through the insulators, and go away from the pole on the other side. Child's play! The covering on the lines is rather tough, however. We shall have to use the wire-cutters."

The Phoenix returned to the top of the pole with

the cutters, and worked on the wires for five more minutes. Bits of debris began to shower down on the hedge. One of the wires vibrated on a low note like a slack guitar string.

"We must not forget the difference between alternating and direct current, my boy," said the Phoenix as it flew down again. "An important problem, that. Where is our wire? Ah, there we are. The pliers, please."

"Do you need any help up there?" David asked.

"No, everything is coming along beautifully, thank you. I shall have everything finished in a flash."

Trailing one end of the wire in its beak, the Phoenix flew up into the darkness once more. The tinkering sounds began again, and a spurt of falling debris rattled in the leaves of the hedge.

Suddenly it happened. There was a terrific burst of blue light, a sharp squawk from the Phoenix, and a shower of sparks. Another blue flash blazed up. The lights in the house, and down the whole street, flickered and went out. In the blackness which followed, each stage of the Phoenix's descent could be heard as clearly as cannon shots: the twanging and snapping as it tumbled through the wires, a drawn-out squawk and the flop of wings in the air below, the crash into the hedge, the

jarring thud against the ground. Broken wires began to
sputter ominously and fire out sparks. A smell of singed
feathers and burning rubber filled the air.

By the light of the sparks David saw the Phoenix
staggering to its feet. He jumped to the bird's side, but
the Phoenix waved him away with its wing.

"Quick, my boy," it gasped. "We must make a strategic retreat! Meet me on the ledge in the morning. Ouch!" The Phoenix beat at the smoldering sparks in its tail and flew off, leaving a trail of acrid smoke hanging in the air.

David had the presence of mind to gather up all the tools, the wire, bell, and pushbutton, and one of the Phoenix's feathers, which had been torn out during the fall. He slipped through a cellar window, hid the equipment under a stack of old boxes, and ran noisily up the stairs into the kitchen.

"Hey!" he shouted. "The lights are out!"

"Is that you, dear?" came Mother's anxious voice from the dining room.

"The telephone's dead!" Dad shouted from the hall.

Aunt Amy came bumping down the stairs with a candle. "It's that burglar!" she cried. "Turning out all the lights so he can murder us in our beds!"

"Look!" David shouted, "the line's broken in our back yard!"

They could hear the wailing of sirens now. Fire trucks, repair trucks, and police cars pulled up in front of the house. Everyone in the block turned out to see what had happened. It took the repair men an hour to untangle the wires and fix them. And all the time policemen were going through the crowd, asking questions and writing things down in their notebooks. They were looking rather haggard, David thought.

8: *In Which David and the Phoenix Visit a Banshee, and a Surprise Is Planted in the Enemy's Camp*

NEXT DAY MOTHER ASKED
David to help her straighten out the garden, which had
been trampled by the repair men; so he could not go to
see the Phoenix until after lunch. But when that was
finished, he rushed up the mountainside as fast as he
could, wondering all the way what he and the Phoenix
were going to do now.

115

The ledge was empty when he got there. He shouted, "Phoenix!" and listened.

"Hel-l-lp!" came a faint answering cry from the other end of the ledge.

David jumped through the thicket. A pitiful sight met his eyes. There was the Phoenix, dangling by one foot from the snare, its wings feebly struggling and its free foot clawing the air. The feathers of its wings and tail were singed. Great beads of sweat rolled from its forehead into a puddle on the ground below. The snared foot was blue and swollen.

"Get me down," gasped the Phoenix weakly.

David took a running leap at the sapling, which broke under the sudden increase of weight, and the two of them crashed to the ground. He unfastened the noose and dragged the Phoenix to the shadiest, softest spot on the ledge.

"Hoist with my own petard," said the Phoenix bitterly. "Rub my foot, will you? Oh dear oh dear oh dear! Hurts."

"What happened?" David asked as he rubbed the swollen foot. "How long have you been caught?"

"Missed my way in the dark," said the Phoenix, wiping its brow. "Thought I was on the other side of the ledge, and landed right on that fool trap. Hung there all night and all morning. Thought you would never come, my boy. Oh dear, oh dear, what a horrible experience! My tail was still on fire when I landed, too. I fully expected to be burned to a crisp." A large tear rolled down the Phoenix's beak.

David murmured soothing words and continued to chafe the Phoenix's foot. "Does it feel any better now?"

"The feeling is coming back, my boy," said the Phoenix, gritting its beak. "Ouch! All pins and needles." It flexed its toes gingerly. "Rub a bit more, please. Gently."

The swelling began to go down. With a handful of damp grass David soothed the marks left by the noose.

"That stupid Electric Company!" the Phoenix suddenly burst out. "Putting everyone in danger with a short-circuited power line! Let this be a lesson to you, my boy. Anything worth doing is worth doing well. They will hear from us, believe me! We shall write them a stiff complaint!"

"Well, Phoenix," said David hopefully, "we can set the snare again if we can find another good sapling; and we still have the other one, so we're pretty well protected. And why couldn't we meet every night by the hedge, the way we did last night? The bell was a good idea, but we *could* get along without it."

The Phoenix sighed. "I suppose you are right, my boy. There is no use crying over spilt milk. One must set one's jaw and — good heavens, my boy! *Duck!*"

The Phoenix threw itself to the ground and wildly motioned to David to do the same. He flattened himself out beside the bird and said, "What is it, Phoenix?"

"Down the mountainside," whispered the Phoenix. "Look! Do not stick your head over too far."

David wormed his way to the edge, peered down, and gasped. Below him, on the grassy slope at the foot of the scarp, was a figure clad in khaki. It was the Scientist.

"Do you think he saw us?" the Phoenix whispered.

"I don't think so," David whispered back. "He's looking off to the left. Oh, Phoenix, what if he comes up here? What'll we do?"

"Listen," hissed the Phoenix, "run down there. Talk to him, lead him away, distract his attention, anything. Only be quick!"

"All right!"

The Phoenix melted into the thicket, and David jumped to his feet. As he dashed down the trail his brain whirled with questions. What should he do? What could he say? How could he lead the Scientist away? Where would the Phoenix go?

In his haste he forgot one important thing. His foot tripped over the pile of grass and leaves on the trail. The released sapling sprang upward, the noose tightened with a cruel jerk around his ankle, and he was snatched into the air. As the blood rushed to his head he lost control of himself and began to struggle wildly and shout at the top of his voice.

The flat dry voice of the Scientist drifted to him as if through a long tunnel. "What's all this? What are you doing here? Who set this snare?"

"Get me down," David choked. "Please!"

A hand seized him by the scruff of the neck. A knife flashed through the air and cut the rope. David landed on his feet, but his legs gave way and he dropped to his knees. He felt dizzy as the blood rushed away from his head again.

The Scientist tilted his sun helmet back and said, "Well, well — David," in a disagreeable tone. His eyes narrowed behind the spectacles. "What is this snare doing here?"

David struggled to his feet and clutched a bush for support. "Thank you for cutting me down," he said.

The cold blue eyes found David's and held them in a hypnotic stare. "What is this trap doing here? Who set it?"

"I — I was coming down the trail and — and — I was caught in it," David stammered.

"You are avoiding my question, young man," said the Scientist. "Who — set — this — snare? Answer me!"

There was a brilliant flash of gold and blue in the sunlight, the whistle of feathers cleaving the air, the sharp *thwock!* of fisted talons striking. The Scientist pitched forward with a surprised grunt and lay still across the trail — and the Phoenix, executing a flip in the air to check its speed, settled down beside David.

"View halloo!" it shouted excitedly. "Yoicks and Tallyho! Did you see that stoop, my boy? By Jove, the best-trained falcon could not have done better! Believe me, I have been saving that blow for a long time! By Jove, what a magnificent stoop! I think I shall take up Scientist-hunting as a regular thing!"

"Thank goodness, Phoenix!" David exclaimed. "Another minute and you would've been too late! But I hope you haven't — hurt him very much."

"Nonsense, my boy," said the Phoenix. "A head so stuffed with scientific fact cannot be injured. He will

come to in a short while." The Phoenix lifted the Scientist's sun helmet and examined the back of his head. "A large lump is developing, my boy. A most pleasant sight! I fear the sun helmet is now useless — crushed like an eggshell." And the Phoenix smiled proudly.

"Well, I hope it isn't serious," David said doubtfully. "Anyway, we'll have to do something."

"Precisely, my boy. But I think we should have a

drink first." The Phoenix detached a canteen from the Scientist's belt and took a deep swig. "Ah, delicious! Our friend is well prepared, my boy." And indeed, the Scientist had all sorts of things with him: a hand-ax, a sheath knife, a compass, a camera, binoculars, a stop watch, notebooks and pencils, a coil of rope, maps. There was also a packet of sandwiches, which the Phoenix opened and began to eat.

"Now, listen, Phoenix, we have to do something."

"Quite right, my boy," the Phoenix mumbled, with its mouth full. "Have a sandwich — spoils of war — peanut butter — very nourishing. The fact is that I have just thought of another plan, which cannot fail. Have we any money left?"

"Yes, four gold pieces. Why?"

"Splendid. Now, my boy, I shall leave you. When the Scientist wakes up, you will help him down to wherever he lives. Find out where his room is. I shall meet you by the hedge at midnight. Be sure you have the gold pieces with you."

"All right. What are we — "

"Sure you will not have a sandwich?"

"No, thank you. What are we — "

"Very well. Farewell, then, my boy. Till midnight."

David poured what was left in the canteen over the Scientist's head and fanned him with a notebook. Presently the man stirred and groaned. Then he sat up and muttered, "What hit me?"

"Can you stand up yet?" David said.

Too dazed to ask any more questions, the Scientist got up, groaning, put on his broken spectacles, collected his scattered equipment, and leaned on David. The two of them proceeded slowly down the trail together, frequently sitting down to rest. The Scientist murmured the name of his hotel and pointed out the direction.

Townspeople stared at them as they passed, but no one stopped them or asked questions, and they reached the hotel without further incident. They entered the lobby, and the Scientist sank into a chair.

"Let me help you to your room," said David.

In a few minutes the Scientist got up again, and they took the elevator to the fourth floor. David closely watched the direction they were going, and when they came into the Scientist's room, he looked quickly through the window. There was a fire escape just outside. He had the information now: fourth floor, west side, fire escape by window.

The Scientist eased himself onto the bed with a groan.

Then he turned to David and said severely: "There's something strange about all this, and I intend to get to the bottom of it. You'll be hearing from me, young man!"

"All right," said David, closing the door. "And you'll be hearing from *us*," he added in an undertone, "if I know the Phoenix!"

Flying at night was colder than flying by day, but it was more thrilling, too. They whistled through an immense blackness. Stars glittered overhead, and quicksilver patches of moonlight and shadow flashed across the clouds below. They were going to Ireland, but why, David did not know. The Phoenix was playing its wait-and-see game again.

In an hour or so they shot out over the edge of the cloud mass, and David could see a rocky coast below, dark and cold in the half-light. The Phoenix began to slant down toward it, and presently they landed in a little meadow. One side of the meadow ran down to a bog filled with reeds, and on the other side was a gloomy wood. Everything was dark and indistinct, but David thought he could tell why the Phoenix had called this the Emerald Isle. The grass beneath their feet was the thickest he had ever felt. He touched a boulder and found it furry with moss. With the wood and the reed-choked bog, the whole place would be rich with various greens in the daylight.

Just then they saw a little man approaching them from the wood. He was three feet tall, dressed all in green, and had a long white beard. When he reached them he raised his cap politely and said, "Good evenin' to you."

"A fine evening to you, my good Leprechaun," said the Phoenix. "Could you kindly tell us — "

"Will you have a cigar?" the Leprechaun interrupted.

With a surprised "Thank you very much," the Phoenix took the cigar, bit off the end, and popped it into its beak. The Leprechaun lighted it, and the Phoenix puffed away.

"Stick o' gum, lad?" said the Leprechaun to David, holding out a pack.

"Why, yes, thank you," said David. He took the stick of gum from the pack, and was immediately sorry for it. The stick was made of wood and had a small wire spring, like a mouse trap, which snapped down on his finger and made him yelp with pain. At the same instant the Phoenix's cigar exploded, knocking the startled bird backwards into a bush.

"Haw haw haw!" shouted the Leprechaun, rolling on the ground and holding his sides. "Haw haw haw!"

In a trice the Phoenix had pounced on the Leprechaun and pinned him to the ground.

"Let him up," said David furiously. "I'll punch his head for him."

"I think, my boy," said the Phoenix coldly, "that I shall carry the creature up into the clouds and drop him. Or should we take him back with us and hand him over to the Scientist?"

"Now, don't take offense, Your Honor," said the Leprechaun. "I thought you'd look at it as kind o' comic."

"Exceedingly comic," said the Phoenix severely. "I am quite overcome with mirth and merriment. But perhaps — *perhaps* — I shall let you off lightly if you tell us where the Banshee lives."

"The — the Banshee of Mare's Nest Wood?"

"The same. Speak!"

A new light of respect and fear came into the Leprechaun's eyes. "She's a terror, she is. What'll you be wanting —"

"None of your business!" roared the Phoenix. "Where is she?"

The Leprechaun had begun to tremble. "Follow the

path yonder through the wood until you reach the cave, Your Honor. You're not friends o' hers, are you? You'll not be telling on me? I'm real sorry for those jokes, Your Honor."

The Leprechaun's fright was so genuine now that the Phoenix relented and let him go. The little creature dashed off like a rabbit into the bog.

"Let that be a lesson to you, my boy," said the Phoenix. "Beware the Leprechaun bearing gifts. But I wonder why the thought of the Banshee frightened him so?"

They followed the path until they came to the mouth of a cave under a heap of rocks. The Phoenix plunged in, and David nervously followed. The cave turned out to be a long passageway which led, after several turns, into a chamber.

From the ceiling of this rocky vault hung an electric light bulb, which glared feebly through drifts of smoke. All around the walls were wooden boxes, stacked up to make shelves and cupboards. These were filled with an astonishing array of objects: bottles, vials, alembics, retorts, test tubes, decanters, cages, boxes, jars, pots, skulls, books, snake skins, wands, waxen images, pins and needles, locks of hair, crystal balls, playing cards, dice, witchhazel forks, tails of animals, spices, bottles of ink in several colors, clay pipes, a small brass scale, compasses, measuring cups, a piggy bank which squealed off and on in a peevish way, balls of string and ribbons, a pile of magazines called *The Warlock Weekly,* a broken ukulele, little heaps of powder, colored stones, candle ends, some potted cacti, and an enormous cash register. In the middle of the chamber a little hideous crone in a Mother Hubbard crouched over a saucepan, stirring it with a wooden spoon. The saucepan was resting in the coals of an open fire, and smoke and steam together spread out in a murky, foul-smelling fog.

The crone peered at them over the top of her spectacles and cackled, "Come in, come in, dearies. I'll be with you as soon as ever I finish this brew."

The Phoenix, who had been gazing around the chamber in surprise, said, "My dear Banshee, since when have you taken up witchcraft? This is most unexpected."

"Ah, 'tis the Phoenix!" exclaimed the hag, peering at them again. "Well, fancy that now! Och, you may well ask, and I'll be telling you. 'Tis a poor life being a Banshee — long hours and not so much as sixpence in it for a full night's work, and I got that sick of it! So I changed me trade. 'Sure, you'll never make a go of it,' they told me, 'and at your age,' they says, 'and once you've got your station in life,' they says, 'there's no changing it.' 'It's in the prime of me life I am,' says I, 'and I'll not be changing me mind for all your cackling,' says I, 'and if certain mouths don't shut up,' says I, 'I'll cast spells that'll make certain people wish they were dead.' *That* set them back on their heels, you may be sure. Well, 'twas the best decision of me life. The money pours in like sorrows to a widow, and I'll be retiring within the year to live out my days like a proper queen."

Then the Banshee caught sight of David and hobbled over to him, peering into his frightened eyes.

"Ah, the wee darling," she crooned, "the plump little mannikin. What a broth he'd make, to be sure." She pinched his arm, and he started back in terror. "So firm and plump, to make the mouth water. Sell him to me, Phoenix!"

"Nonsense," said the Phoenix sharply. "What we desire — "

At this instant the contents of the saucepan began to hiss and bubble. "Whoops, dearies, the brew is boiling!" shrieked the Banshee, and she hobbled back to the fire to resume her work. She looked in a recipe book, stirred, clapped her hands, sang hair-raising incantations in a quavery voice, and added a pinch of salt and sulfur. She

sprinkled spices from a shaker, waved her wand, popped
in a dead toad, and fanned up the fire with an ostrich
plume.

"Now for the hard part," she said, grinning at them
toothlessly. She measured out a spoonful of green powder, weighed it in the scales, and flung it into the saucepan. There was a loud explosion. A huge blast of steam
flared out and engulfed them. When it had cleared, they

saw the Banshee tilting the saucepan over a small bottle. One ruby drop of fluid fell into the bottle. It darted forth rays of light as it fell, and tinkled like a silver coin rolling down flights of marble steps.

The Banshee corked the bottle and held it up proudly to the light. "Will you look at that, now?" she crooned. "The finest ever I brewed. Ah, the mystic droplet! Some swain will be buying that, now, and putting it in a lassie's cup o' tea, and she'll be pining away for love of him before the day's out."

She put the bottle on the shelf, pasted a label on it, and turned to them with a businesslike air.

"Now, dearies, what'll you be wanting? Philtres? Poison? — I've a special today, only five shillings a vial. A spell? What about your fortunes? — one shilling if seen in the crystal ball, one and six if read from the palm. A hex? — I've the finest in six counties. A ticket to the Walpurgis Night Ball?"

"We want a Wail," said the Phoenix. "And we shall accept nothing but the best and loudest you have."

"Ah, a Banshee's Wail, is it?" cried the hag. "You've come to the right shop, dearies, to be sure. Now, let me see . . ." She hobbled to a shelf which contained a row of boxes, ran her finger along them, stopped at one, and took it down. "Here we are — key of C-sharp, two minutes long, only five shillings threepence."

"No, no," said the Phoenix. "A larger one. We have something more than mice to frighten."

"A bigger one? Och, here's a lovely one, now — five minutes long, ascending scale with a sob at the end, guaranteed to scare a statue. Yours for ten and six. I call that a real bargain, now!"

"Bah!" said the Phoenix impatiently. "Enough of these squeaks! We want a real *Wail*, my dear Banshee — such a Wail as never before was heard on the face of this earth. And stop this babbling about shillings and pence. We are prepared to pay in gold." The Phoenix took the four pieces of gold from David and carelessly tossed them into the air.

The Banshee's eyes flew wide open, and she twirled herself around like a top. "Och, the sweet music of its tinkling!" she exclaimed. "The lovely sheen of light upon it! *There's* a sight for eyes used to naught but silver! Ah, but dearies, I've no Wail worth four pieces of gold. I'll have to make one up special." She hobbled rapidly around the chamber until she had found a box as large as a bird cage, and an ear trumpet. She opened the box, shook it to make sure it was empty, and put in two heads of cabbage. ("Such monstrous appetites these Wails do have!" she explained.) She fastened the lid carefully with a catch-lock, and inserted the ear trumpet in a hole in one side of the box. Then she disappeared through a sound-proof door, which they had not seen before on account of the smoke.

Fifteen minutes later the Banshee came out with the box, plugging up the hole in its side with a bit of wax.

133

She was pale and trembling, and beads of sweat covered her face. She smiled weakly at them, seized an earthenware jug, and drained it in one gulp. The color began to return to her face.

"Wsssht!" she gasped, wiping her brow with the sleeve of her Mother Hubbard. "Ah, dearies, that was the effort of me life! 'Tis a Wail to make one burst with pride, though I do say it meself. Thirteen minutes long by the clock, with a range of ten octaves! 'Twould frighten the Old Nick himself!"

"Splendid!" said the Phoenix. "The fact is, I sometimes suspect that that is precisely with whom we are dealing at home."

The light suddenly dawned on David. "Phoenix!" he cried. "I bet we're going to give the Wail to the Scientist!"

"Precisely, my boy!" The Phoenix beamed.

"Oh, golly golly golly!" David sang as he danced around.

"And I'll guarantee it, dearies!" the Banshee cackled. "One hundred per cent satisfaction or your money back!"

"Defeat and confusion to the enemy!" the Phoenix shouted, giving the special squawk which was its battle cry.

The Banshee received her gold. The Phoenix told David for goodness sake not to drop the box or let the lid pop open, or they would regret it to their dying day. David, hearing the rustle of the Wail as it ravenously attacked the cabbages inside the box, assured the Phoenix that he would be careful. The Banshee said, "Ah, Phoenix, do sell the laddie to me," but her tone was more teasing than serious, and they all laughed. Good-bys were said all round, and David and the Phoenix left. The last thing they heard as they felt their way up the dark passage was the happy cackling of the Banshee and the clang of the cash register.

They got back to the hotel before dawn and very carefully crept down the fire escape into the Scientist's room. They put the box on the bedside table, stuck out their tongues at the sleeping Scientist, and crept out again. Then they went home, the Phoenix to the ledge and David to bed, where he fell asleep instantly.

The Wail was wildly successful. The Scientist released it from its box at seven o'clock in the morning. People living in the hotel thought the world had come to its end. The rest of the town wondered if it was a riot, or an earthquake, or both with three steam calliopes thrown in for good measure. David, who lived twelve blocks from the hotel, stirred in his sleep and dreamed he was riding a fire engine. Even the Phoenix claimed later that a kind of moan was borne on the breeze all the way up to the ledge.

The hotel burst into activity like a kicked anthill. People poured down the fire escapes, shot out through the doors, lowered themselves into the street with ropes of knotted blankets. Others barricaded themselves in their rooms by piling furniture against the doors and windows. One guest found his way to the cellar and hid in an ash can for two days. The manager crawled into the office safe and locked the door, without even bothering to remember that he was the only one who knew the combination. The telephone exchange was jammed as calls flooded in to mobilize the Boy Scouts, the Red Cross, the Salvation Army, the National Guard, and the Volunteer Flood Control Association. When the Wail finally died out (which was not until seven-thirty, because it had devoured both cabbages during the night and had grown to more than twice its original size) the police entered the hotel in force, armed to the eyebrows. They found nothing. At the end of a three-hour search the Chief handed in his resignation.

As for the Scientist, he disappeared completely. A farmer living three miles out of town said he saw a man, dressed in a nightshirt and head-bandage, running down the valley road. The farmer guessed the man's speed to be thirty-five miles an hour. But, he added, there was such a cloud of dust being raised that he could not see very well.

"It might have been fifty miles an hour," he said.

No one doubted him.

9: *In Which David and the Phoenix Call On a Faun, and a Lovely Afternoon Comes to a Strange End*

THE PHOENIX WAS DEAD
tired. And no wonder — all in one week it had escaped
from Gryffons, raced with a Witch, made round-trip
flights to the Pacific Isles and Ireland, been caught in a
snare, got burned by a short circuit, and been knocked
down by an exploding cigar. Even a bird as strong as the
Phoenix cannot do all these things without needing a rest.

So the traveling part of David's education was stopped for a while to let the Phoenix recover.

The days went by pleasantly on the ledge. Summer was at its height. The sun fell on them with just the right amount of warmth as they lolled on the grass. The air was filled with a lazy murmuring. "Listen," the murmuring seemed to say, "don't talk, don't think — close your eyes and listen." Below them, the whole valley danced and wavered in the heat waves, so that it seemed to be under water.

There were long, lazy conversations that began nowhere and ended nowhere — the wonderful kind in which you say whatever comes to your head without fear of being misunderstood, because what you say has little importance anyway. The Phoenix told of the times and adventures it had had. Of the forgotten corners of the world where life went on as it had from the beginning, and of friends who lived there. Of Trolls who mined metal from the earth and made from it wondrous machines which whirred and clattered and clanked and did absolutely nothing. ("The best kind of machine after all, my boy, since they injure no one, and there is nothing to worry about when they break down.") Of Unicorns ("Excellent chaps, but so frightfully melancholy") which shone white in the sun and tossed their ivory horns like rapiers. Of a Dragon who, having no treasure to guard, got together a pathetic heap of colored pebbles in its cave. ("And really, he came to believe in time that they were absolutely priceless, and went about with a worried frown of responsibility on his brow!") David, in turn, told the Phoenix about the games he used to play when he lived in the flat country, and all about school, and Mother and Dad and Aunt Amy and Beckie.

He could not help laughing now and then over the Scientist's defeat. But whenever this came up, the Phoenix would shake its head with a kind of sad wisdom.

"My boy, there are certain things, such as head colds and forgetting where you have left your keys, which are inevitable — and I am afraid that the Scientist is, too."

"Oh, Phoenix, you don't think he'll come back, do you?"

"Yes, my boy, I do. I can see the whole train of events: He will recover from his fright. He will be curious about the Wail, and will return to investigate it. Once here, he will remember us, and we shall have to take him into account once more."

"Oh. Do you think it'll happen soon?"

"Oh, no, my boy, nothing to worry about for the

time being. But we must remember that it will happen some day."

"Yes, I guess you're right. I think he's hateful!"

"I cannot disagree with you there, my boy. Of course, I have no doubt that, in general, the advancement of science is all to the good. Knowledge is power. But on days like this I sometimes wonder . . . Does it not seem to you that the highest aim in life at the moment is to enjoy the sunlight and allow others to do the same?"

"You're right, Phoenix — but then, you always are. I was just thinking the same thing. It's funny . . . I mean . . . well, *you* know. Why can't people leave other people alone — and — and — well, just *enjoy* themselves and lie in the sun and listen to the wind?"

"That is the way of the world, my boy. Getting and spending, and all that sort of thing. But come! Why should we worry over the follies of the rest of the world? A day like this was made for living, not thinking. Begone, dull care!"

And they would forget the Scientist and watch a pair of butterflies chase each other instead.

But one day the Phoenix suddenly stood up with a startled expression on its face. "My dear chap!" it exclaimed. "I have just remembered! Tomorrow . . ."

"What about tomorrow?"

"Why, my boy, tomorrow another century rounds its mark. To be brief, tomorrow is my birthday. My five hundredth birthday."

"Well, congratulations, Phoenix!"

"Thank you, my boy. Five hundred . . . Destiny . . . Have I mentioned before, my boy, that I have a magnificent destiny?"

"No. What is it, Phoenix?"

"I — well, it is strange, my boy, but I do not know . . . but that it is magnificent no one can doubt."

"Do I have one too?"

"Of course, my boy. We all do."

David was glad of that. He did not know exactly what a destiny was, however, and he tried to think of how one would look. But the only picture which came to his mind was that of a small, mousy creature (his destiny) looking up in admiration to a splendid thing of flame and gold, dazzling to the eyes — the Phoenix's mysterious destiny.

He said, "We'll have to do something special tomorrow to celebrate, Phoenix."

The Phoenix looked thoughtful. "I think we had better do whatever we are going to do *today*," it said.

"Well, we can do something today *and* tomorrow, then," said David. "After all, a birthday only comes once a year, and it seems a shame to spend only one day on it. Especially when it's a five hundredth birthday."

"Tomorrow . . ." said the Phoenix doubtfully. "I have a strange feeling, my boy — for once, I find myself unable to explain — most odd, *most* odd . . . five hundredth birthday . . ."

"Ah, well," it went on more cheerfully, "I shall undoubtedly remember later. The pressing question is, what shall we do now?"

David got up, thought for a while, and suddenly flung his arms wide. "Oh, Phoenix," he cried, "it's such a beautiful day, I wish it could go on forever! Couldn't we go somewhere — somewhere where we — oh, I don't know. I can't explain it. Anywhere *you* say, Phoenix."

The Phoenix looked at him for a long time. "I think I understand, my boy. Yes . . . How about one of the forgotten places I told you about? Would you like to meet a Faun?"

It was a green valley, completely enclosed by the barren mountains which towered above it. At one end a waterfall hung on the face of a cliff, a misty thread pouring into a rainbow-arched pool. A brook serpentined through fields and groves of trees. There were flocks of sheep and goats in the fields. Here and there were strange ruins of marble and red granite — columns, peristyles, benches carved with lions' heads, and pedestals.

They landed in a little glade, and David got down in silent wonderment. The very stillness of the air was enchanted. The grass, dappled with sun and shadow, wore a mantle of flowers. Clouds of butterflies sprang up at their approach and swirled about them. To their right stood two broken columns, half-hidden beneath a wild tangle of vine and clusters of purple grapes. Beyond was the forest, dark and cool and silent, with shafts of sunlight in it like golden spears pinning the forest floor to earth. There was no breeze. And as David stood there, scarcely daring to breathe, they heard the sound of shepherd pipes coming from the edge of the wood. It was a minor tune, but somehow lilting too, with the rippling of water in it, and the laughter of birds flying high, and the whisper of reeds as they bend together by the edge of streams, and the gaiety of crickets by night, and the pouring of summer rain.

The piping died away, and the Phoenix beckoned to the spellbound David. Together they walked across the glade, leaving behind them a wake of swirling butter-flies. An immense oak stood at the edge of the forest. At its foot, on a bed of moss, sat the Faun.

He was the same size as David. From the waist down he was covered with shaggy hair like a goat's, and instead of feet he had cloven hooves. The hair on his head was black and curly, and tumbled around small pointed ears and a pair of short horns. His eyes were slanted slightly upward, and he had a pointed chin and a snub nose.

The Faun waved his pipes saucily at the Phoenix and gave a wry smile. "Hullo, Phoenix! Back again to honor us with your wit and wisdom? What gems of advice have you got for us now?"

"My dear Faun," said the Phoenix stiffly, "I have brought my friend David, who is acquiring an education. We — "

The Faun smiled at David. "Want to race?" he said.

"Sure," said David. "Where to?"

"One moment," harrumphed the Phoenix. "What we — "

"Down to that pedestal and back," said the Faun.

"All right. Wait till I tie my shoe."

The Phoenix harrumphed again. "This is all very well in its place, but we *should* — "

"Ready?" said the Faun. "One, two, three, *go!*"

They dashed for the stone marker. It was an even race until they reached the pedestal, but there David tried to turn without slowing down, slipped on the grass, and went sprawling on his hands and knees. The Faun knew better. He sprang at the pedestal with both hooves, bounced from it like a spring, and began to race back to the oak. But then he too fell, tripping over a vine, and David shot past him and touched the oak one jump ahead of him, shouting "First!"

They sat down on the moss, panting. The Faun said, "You can really run! I'm sorry you fell."

"Well, you fell too, so that makes us even," said David. They looked at each other and for some reason burst out laughing. They rolled around on the moss and laughed until tears came, while the Phoenix fidgeted in reproachful silence.

When they had calmed down a little, the Faun said, "Can you dance?"

"No," said David. "I wish I could, though."

"The educational value of dancing is practically nil," the Phoenix began severely. "I advise — "

"Sure you can dance," said the Faun. "Listen." He brought the pipes to his lips and began to play.

And much to his surprise and delight, David found himself dancing as though he had never done anything else in his life. The wonderful thing was that he did not have to think about what he was doing: the music was doing it all for him. He saw that even the Phoenix was shuffling around in time to the piping, and looking very embarrassed about it, too.

"There," said the Faun when they had finished, "you *can* dance, and very well. Even old Phoenix can dance." Suddenly he jumped up and cried, "Let's go — come on!" and started to run.

David followed, not knowing where they were going

147

and not caring. The Phoenix came after them, half running and half flying to keep up. They raced across the glade, through a stand of trees, and out into the meadow beyond. There they came to a bank of daisies, and threw themselves into the middle of it and began to pelt each other with blossoms. The Phoenix, finally caught up in the spirit of it, collected a huge bunch while they were wrestling, flew suddenly over them, and drowned them beneath a deluge of flowers. Near by was the stream. They splashed in the shallows, skipped pebbles over the surface, and dug a harbor with two dikes in the sandy part of the shore. The Faun showed David how to build little boats of reeds, and the Phoenix made them sail by blowing up a wind with its wings.

They had a tree-climbing contest, which David won because his feet were better than hooves for standing on branches. But the Faun won the jumping contest because of the tremendous spring in his legs. They came out even in the handstand, somersault, and skin-the-cat contest. And the Phoenix won when they played skip-rope with a piece of vine, because it could hover in the air with its wings while the vine swished over and under.

They had fun with the sheep and goats, too. The Faun made the animals dance and caper to a tune from his pipes, and showed David how to ride on the rams. You crept up very quietly from behind — jumped suddenly on their backs — got a quick grip around their necks — and away in a rush! It was almost as good as flying, except that you got jolted off sooner or later. Then watch out! — it took some quick dodging to escape the horns of the angry rams. They left the goats alone, because of their sharper horns and the wicked look in their eyes.

"I know where some pictures are," said the Faun. "Come on!" And he led them to a kind of glade ringed with shattered columns. The ground there was covered with moss and drifts of leaves. They each got a stick to clear away the debris, and uncovered a beautiful mosaic pavement. It was made of bits of colored stone and tile, which were arranged to make pictures. There were scenes of youths treading out wine, minstrels with lyres, gods with curly hair, and a beast which was half man and half horse. There were maidens dancing to flute and drums, hunters battling with boars and lions, warriors clashing with sword and shield and spear. There were series of pictures telling stories of wonders and adventures in far-distant lands, voyages, wars, conquests. The Faun proudly pointed out a picture of other Fauns dancing with

Nymphs. The Phoenix gazed very thoughtfully at some scenes of a bird building and sitting in a nest of flames. But the last pictures of this story had been broken up by roots, so they could not see how it ended.

When they came to the end of the valley, where the rainbow arched over the pool, David told them of the pot of gold which is supposed to be at the foot of rainbows. They looked for it, but without success, because the rainbow disappeared whenever they got too close to it. So David and the Faun contented themselves with jumping into the pool and ducking each other and making bubbly noises, while the Phoenix, who could not swim, stood on the shore and beamed at them. They picked ferns from under the waterfall and made wreaths and garlands, which they threw at the Phoenix's head like quoits. The Faun showed them a certain place to shout from if you wanted to hear an echo. The Phoenix shouted, "A stitch in time saves nine!" and the echo dolorously answered, "A switch is fine for crime."

Wet and tired from splashing in the pool, they stretched out in the sun to dry. A grapevine grew near them, and they gorged themselves on the fruit, smearing their faces and hands with purple. And David closed his eyes and thought, "Now I'm having a dream, and so is the

Phoenix. We're all dreaming the same thing and living in the dream, and I wish — oh, I wish none of us will ever wake up!"

But he had just opened his eyes again when the Faun leaped to his feet and cried "Listen!" and flicked his pointed ears forward like a cat.

David stood up and said in a puzzled voice, "I don't hear anything." He noticed that the Phoenix had also got up, and was listening uncomfortably to whatever it was.

"Listen! Oh, listen!" cried the Faun. There was a joyous light in his eyes as he leaned forward with his lips slightly parted, straining toward the mysterious silence. Suddenly he shouted, "I'm coming, I'm coming!" and dashed off into the wood.

"Good heavens," muttered the Phoenix. "I had forgotten about — this. Let us go home, my boy."

A strange, uncontrollable trembling had seized David's legs. He still could hear nothing, but some feeling, some hint of an unknown, tremendous event hung quivering in the air about them and sent little electric thrills racing up and down his whole body.

"Oh, Phoenix, what is it, what is it?" he whispered.

"I think we had best be going, my boy," said the Phoenix anxiously. "Come along."

"Phoenix — " But he heard it now. It came whispering toward them, the sound of pipes caroling — pipes
such as the Faun had played, but greater, as an organ is
greater than a flute. The wild, sweet sound rose and fell,
swelled like a full choir, diminished into one soprano
voice that pierced David through and through, caressing
and tugging, calling, "Come . . . come . . . run . . .
run . . ."

"Phoenix!" David cried. "Oh, Phoenix, listen, listen!"

"Run . . . run . . ." the pipes whispered.

"Let us go home, my boy," said the Phoenix warn-
ingly.

"Come . . . come . . ." cried the pipes.

They could be resisted no longer. In a transport of
joy, David shouted "I'm coming!" and raced away toward
the sound. There was nothing in his mind now, nothing
in the whole world, but a desire to be near those pipes.
He must run like the winds, leap and shout, roll in the
grass, throw himself down flowered slopes, follow that
magic music wherever it should lead. He fled blindly
through the wood, heedless of the branches which
whipped his face and the thorns which tore at his legs.
The pipes were calling more loudly now: "Run . . .

run . . . faster . . . faster . . ." Then the Phoenix plunged to earth in front of him, threw out both wings, and shouted "Stop!"

"Let me go, Phoenix!" David cried. "Let me by! I want to run, I must run!"

He made a desperate effort to push past the outstretched wings. But the Phoenix flung him to the ground, picked him up before he could kick once, and threw him on its back. Then they were flying at full speed, dodging through gaps in the branches and between close-set trunks, with leaves and twigs slashing them from every side. They burst out of the wood and sped over a meadow. David saw below them a huge Faun-like figure pacing majestically across the sward. A flaming wreath encircled its brow, garlands of flowers hung from its arms and shoulders, and those enchanted pipes were lifted to its lips. Around the cloven hooves, and trailing out behind, danced a multitude of creatures — lambs and kids gamboling, goats and rams tossing their horns, foxes, furry waves of squirrels, rabbits kicking up their heels, Fauns and Nymphs rollicking, frogs and crickets and serpents. Above them flew birds and butterflies and beetles and bats in swirling clouds. Full-voiced, the glorious pipes sang. "Come, come, run, run! Follow, leap and dance,

adore and obey! Run, oh, run, heed me before all passes!
Follow, before it is too late, too late, too late . . ."

And David, in a delirium of desire, shouted "I'm coming!" and jumped from the Phoenix's back.

For an instant, as he fell through the air, he thought he would succeed in joining the dancing throng. But the Phoenix, plunging after him falconwise with folded wings, seized his collar in its talons, and snatched him up from the very arms of the Faun, who had recognized him and called his name as he fell.

Up toward the cloudless sky they soared. David cried, pleaded, pommeled the Phoenix with his fists. The Phoenix ignored his struggling and continued to climb with tremendous wing strokes. Up and up and up . . . The piping grew fainter in the distance, its magic weakened. The enchanted dancers diminished into specks, the valley fell away until it was only a green splash nestled among the jagged peaks. And David burst into tears . . . and then wondered why he was crying . . . and tried to remember, and could not. The trembling left his body, and he dangled limply. His eyes closed.

10: *In Which a Five Hundredth Birthday Is Celebrated, and the Phoenix Bows to Tradition*

"THAT'S FUNNY," SAID David, rubbing his eyes and looking around in a puzzled way. "Where are we, Phoenix?"

" 'Home is the sailor, home from the hill,' " the Phoenix said, " 'And the hunter home from the sea.' Or is it the other way around? At any rate, we are home, my boy."

And so they were.

"Weren't we playing with a Faun just now?"

"Quite so."

"But there was something else," David said. "Something . . . Didn't somebody say, 'Follow, before it is too late,' or something like that? *Did* we follow? — I can't remember."

"No, my boy. By the time one hears that, it is already too late."

"Oh." Too late for what? he wondered. Oh, well . . . He sighed, and fell to daydreaming.

A cough from the Phoenix brought him back.

"Beg your pardon?"

"I have never seen you so thoughtful, my boy. However, I believe I know what you are thinking about. It *is* a difficult problem, is it not?"

"Yes, I was just — "

" — thinking what you could get me for a birthday present," interrupted the Phoenix. "Am I not correct?"

David, who had not even given this a thought until now, flushed.

"Aha!" said the Phoenix triumphantly. "Just as I thought! Believe me, my dear fellow, when you have been around as long as *I* have, you can read the minds of your friends as easily as a book. Now, the problem of what to give is a hard one at any time, but the problem of what to give for a five hundredth birthday is even harder. A monogrammed ash tray? I do not receive cigars often enough to make that practical. A hand-knitted sweater? It would not fit (they never do). A gold-plated watch chain? I have no watch. No, the best idea would be to get me something which I can use."

"Certainly, Phoenix," David stammered. "What *do* you want, then?"

"Ah! We have reached the kernel of the problem. And the answer, my boy, is this: cinnamon."

"Cinnamon?"

"Precisely. Also a box of matches — the kind that strike anywhere, you know."

"Well — all right. It doesn't sound like much of a present, but if that's what you really want . . . What are you going to do with them, Phoenix? I mean, if you don't mind my asking."

"The plain fact is, my boy," said the Phoenix doubtfully, "the plain fact is — well, I do not know. Odd! But something tells me I shall need them. Well, it will come to me in the morning, no doubt. And then, of course, I shall be very glad to have them on hand."

"All right, cinnamon and matches, then. And I'll get some — no, I won't tell you *that*. It'll be a surprise."

"A surprise? Splendid, my boy! You could not, I suppose, drop me a small hint? No? But of course not — one hint and my powerful Intellect could guess everything — and then the surprise would be spoiled. Well, until tomorrow, then!"

That evening David shut himself in his room and robbed his bank. It was a squat, cast-iron box, with "A Penny Saved Is A Penny Earned" in raised letters on one side. The only way to open it was to smash it with a crowbar, but it could be emptied. It had to be tilted just so, with a knife blade in the slot to catch the coins and guide

them out. This is what David did, with a bread knife borrowed from the kitchen. It was a slow, uncertain job, and one coin (he guessed it was a dime by the way it rattled) never did come out. But the rest, which included his change from Uncle Charles's present, would be enough.

Early next morning he went to the store and bought three large boxes of stick cinnamon, two cans of powdered cinnamon, and a huge box of matches. For the surprise he got a whole quart of strawberry ice cream, with a piece of dry ice to keep it from melting. He wanted to buy a cake, too, and candles, but there was not enough money left. Then he remembered that a new batch of cookies had been baked at home yesterday, which would have to do instead. He wrapped the cinnamon and matches up in a neat package with white paper, tied it in a blue ribbon, and wrote on it "To Feenix, Happy 500 Birthday, from David." Then he took all the cookies from the jar, borrowed two plates and spoons, put everything into a large paper bag, and set out for the Phoenix's ledge.

He was surprised to find the Phoenix working busily in the middle of a wide place on the ledge. Apparently the bird had been at it all night, for a huge pile of sticks and brush had been heaped up on the ground and shaped roughly like a nest. Right now the Phoenix was struggling with a small log, trying to get it on the pile.

"Hello, Phoenix! Happy birthday!"

"Ah, there, my boy! Thank you very much. Could you kindly give me a hand with this log?"

They heaved and grunted the piece of wood to the top of the pile, and David said, "What's this for, Phoenix?"

"This, my boy, is a pyre. A bit untidy around the edges, but nonetheless a pyre."

"Oh," said David. "What's that?"

"Well — a *pyre*, you know — a sort of fire, as it were."

"Oh, *fire*. I thought you said — oh, yes. Fire. Isn't it awfully *warm* for a fire?"

"The weather *is* unusually tropical," said the Phoenix, cocking one eye toward the sun. "This fire, however, is necessary — but I shall explain later. Meanwhile, if you will just aid me with this branch — " And for the next fifteen minutes they worked over the heap, adding to it and shaping it up. David kept his thoughts to himself. He could see that the Phoenix knew what it was doing, so everything must be all right.

"By the way, my boy," said the Phoenix casually, when they had finished, "my prediction was correct. I knew it would be. The inevitable has occurred."

"What are you talking about, Phoenix?"

"The Scientist, my boy. He is in our midst once more."

David clutched a branch in the heap and said "Oh, Phoenix!" in a frightened voice.

"Now, my dear fellow, there is no cause for alarm. He is not nearby at present. I sent him back."

"Sent him back? How?"

"Nothing to it, my boy," said the Phoenix smugly. "He was up at the crack of dawn, toiling with typical stupidity in full sight on the slope below. He was making a blind of green branches to hide in while he spies on me. (Really, the childishness of his efforts! To think for a minute he could fool *me* with such tricks!) Well, I waited until he had gone down the slope to cut more greenery, and when his back was turned, I slipped down to the blind and took his binoculars."

"But Phoenix, what did you want with his binoculars?"

"I did not want his binoculars, my boy, but *he* did. His language when he discovered the loss was simply frightful — I could hear it all the way up here. Of course, he had to return to town for another pair."

"But he'll be back!"

"Precisely, my boy. But he will have something to keep him busy when he returns. I took the liberty of destroying his blind. *That* will hold him."

"But it won't hold him long, Phoenix! We've got to think of something else. Now your whole birthday is spoiled!"

"On the contrary, my boy, it will hold him long enough. Now please do not ask me why; you must take my word for it, and I shall explain later. And my birthday is *not* spoiled. I am looking forward with a great deal of pleasure to the surprise which you promised me. Come, let us enjoy it, whatever it is, and forget the Scientist."

"Well . . . are you *sure* about the Scientist?"

"Absolutely."

The Phoenix was so positive that David began to feel better. He picked up the paper bag and said: "Well, it isn't much of a surprise, really — just a birthday party. And your present. But I think the present should come after the party, don't you?"

"Quite so, my boy. But I shall leave the management of the whole affair in your capable hands."

"All right," said David. "Now, you'll have to turn around, Phoenix, and not look while I'm getting it ready."

The Phoenix obediently turned around, clasping its wings behind its back, and tried hard not to peek. David set the party things out on the grass: ice cream in the middle, the cookies in a ring around it, plates on either side, and spoons beside the plates. He set the Phoenix's present off to one side, where it could be reached when they had finished.

"All right, Phoenix, you can turn around now."

The Phoenix took a long look at everything, and said huskily: "My dear chap, this is quite the nicest moment of my life. How can I possibly thank you?"

They sat down in their places. David passed the cookies and served the ice cream, and said that as far as he was concerned, this was the best birthday party he had ever been to. And the Phoenix said, "Quite so, my boy, but might I make so bold as to ask why?" And David answered, "Well, the reason is that usually during birthday parties you have to play stupid games, like pin-the-tail-on-the-donkey and button-button-who-has-the-button, in spite of the fact that eating good things is the real reason for having a party, as everybody knows." And the Phoenix said, "Precisely, my boy, but people have somehow lost the main idea of the thing. When you come right down to it, ice cream is the basis of any sensible party, and everything else is a waste of time." And David said, "Yes, Phoenix, but don't forget cake and cookies, and candy and nuts and things. They're not as good as ice cream, but they're not a complete waste of time, either." And the Phoenix said, "Of course not, my dear fellow, they are important too. And speaking of ice cream, have you noticed that, while chocolate is very good, and vanilla enjoys great popularity, still there is *nothing* like strawberry?" And David said, "Yes, you're right" — rather sadly, because the Phoenix was eating most of it.

At last the ice cream carton was empty and all the cookies were gone. They both sighed regretfully and brushed away the crumbs. And the Phoenix looked hopefully at the present David had brought.

"Happy birthday, Phoenix," David said, and he handed the gift over with a little bow.

"Thank you, my boy, thank you." The Phoenix opened the package eagerly and gave a pleased cry. *"Just what I wanted, my dear chap!"*

"I'm glad you like it," David said. "Do you know yet what it's for? Can you really use it for something?"

The Phoenix suddenly stopped smiling and looked at

David with a strange expression on its face — an expression David had never seen there before. A vague dread swept through him, and he faltered, "Phoenix . . . you *do* know what it's for? What is it? Tell me."

"Well, my boy — well, the fact *is* — yes, I do know. It came to me this morning while I was constructing the — ah — nest, here. I am afraid it will be a bit hard to explain. The cinnamon — ah — the cinnamon — well, cinnamon *branches* are what I should really have . . ."

"But Phoenix, what's it *for?*"

"Behold, my boy." The Phoenix opened the boxes, and spread the cinnamon sticks on the nest. Then it took the cans and sprinkled the cinnamon powder over the top and sides of the heap, until the whole nest was a brick-dust red.

"There we are, my boy," said the Phoenix sadly. "The traditional cinnamon pyre of the Phoenix, celebrated in song and story."

And with the third mention of the word "pyre," David's legs went weak and something seemed to catch in his throat. He remembered now where he had heard that word before. It was in his book of explorers, and it meant — it meant —

"Phoenix," he choked, "wh-wh-who is the pyre for?"

"For myself," said the Phoenix.

"*Phoenix!*"

"Now, I implore you — please — oh, dear, I *knew* it would be difficult to explain. Look at me, my boy."

David did as he was told, although his eyes were filled with tears and he could not see through the blur.

"Now," said the Phoenix gently, "the fact is that I have, besides my unusually acute Intellect, an Instinct. This Instinct told me that it was my birthday today. It also told me to build this nest of cinnamon. Now it tells me that I must make this nest my pyre, because that is what the Phoenix does at the end of five hundred years. Now, please, my boy! — I admit it does not appear to be a very joyful way of celebrating, but it must be done. This is the traditional end of the Phoenix, my boy, and we cannot ignore the tradition, no matter what our feelings may be. Do you see?"

"No!" David cried. "Please, Phoenix, don't do it! It's horrible! I won't let you do it!"

"But I must, my dear chap! I cannot help it. This is what it means to be the Phoenix. Nothing can stop the tradition. Please, my boy, do not take on so! It is not in the least horrible, I assure you. My Instinct tells me so."

"You said you were going to give me an education,"

David sobbed. "You said we would see — you said — and we've only been on four adventures — you never told me about this — "

"I am terribly sorry, my boy. I could not tell you about it because I did not *know* about it until now. As for your education, it is a pity to have it cut short in this way. I had great plans . . . But consider — you have had four adventures which no one else in the whole world has had! And besides, my boy, we shall see each other again. I do not know how or where, but I am positive of it." The Phoenix flicked a tear from its eye with the tip of one wing, while with the other it patted David awkwardly on the shoulder.

"Don't go, Phoenix, *please* don't go."

"I must, my boy. Here, permit me to present you with a small token (ouch!) of our friendship."

Dimly, through his tears, David saw the Phoenix pluck the longest, bluest feather from its tail, and he felt it being pressed into his hand.

"Good-by, David," said the Phoenix gruffly.

David could stand it no longer. He turned and rushed blindly from the Phoenix, blundered into the thicket, and dropped to the ground with his head buried in his arms. Behind him he heard the sticks snapping as the Phoenix mounted its pyre. A match rasped against the box. The first tongue of flame sizzled in the branches. David pressed his hands over his ears to shut out the sound, but he could feel the heat of the flames as they sprang up. And the noise would not be shut out. It grew and grew, popping, crackling, roaring, until it seemed to fill the world . . .

Perhaps he fainted. Or perhaps from numbness he slipped into a kind of deep sleep. Whichever it was, he returned to consciousness again suddenly. His hands had slipped from his ears, and a sound had brought him back. He lifted his head and listened. The fire had burnt itself out now. The only noise was the hiss and pop of dying embers. But these sounds were too gentle to have awakened him — it must have been something else. Yes — it was a voice. He could hear it quite plainly now. There were angry shouts coming from somewhere below the ledge.

Carefully avoiding the sight of the pyre, David crawled to the edge and glanced over. Far down, on the slope at the foot of the scarp, was a tiny figure dancing and bellowing with rage. The Scientist had returned and discovered the ruins of his blind. David watched him dully. No need to worry about *him* any more. How harm-less he looked now, even ridiculous! David turned away.

He noticed then that he was holding something in his hand, something soft and heavy. As he lifted it to look more closely, it flashed in the sunlight. It was the feather the Phoenix had given him, the tail feather. Tail feather? . . . But the Phoenix's tail had been a sapphire blue. The feather in his hand was of the purest, palest gold.

There was a slight stir behind him. In spite of him-self, he glanced at the remains of the pyre. His mouth dropped open. In the middle of the white ashes and glowing coals there was movement. Something within was struggling up toward the top. The noises grew stronger and more definite. Charred sticks were being snapped, ashes kicked aside, embers pushed out of the way. Now, like a plant thrusting its way out of the soil, there appeared something pale and glittering, which nodded in the breeze. Little tongues of flame, it seemed, licking out into the air . . . No, not flames! A crest of golden feathers! . . . A heave from below lifted the ashes in the center of the pile, a fine cloud of flakes swirled up into the breeze, there was a flash of sunlight glinting on brilliant plumage. And from the ruins of the pyre stepped forth a magnificent bird.

It was the Phoenix, it must be the Phoenix! But it was a new and different Phoenix. It was young and wild, with a fierce amber eye; its crest was tall and proud, its body the slim, muscular body of a hunter, its wings narrow and long and pointed like a falcon's, the great beak and talons razor-sharp and curving. And all of it, from crest to talons, was a burnished gold that reflected the sun in a thousand dazzling lights.

The bird stretched its wings, shook the ash from its tail, and began to preen itself. Every movement was like the flash of a silent explosion.

"Phoenix," David whispered. "Phoenix."

The bird started, turned toward him, looked at him for an instant with wild, fearless eyes, then continued its preening. Suddenly it stopped and cocked its head as if listening to something. Then David heard it too: a shout down the mountainside, louder and clearer now, excited and jubilant. He shivered and looked down. The Scientist was tearing up the goat trail as fast as his long legs would carry him — and he was waving a rifle.

"Phoenix!" David cried. "Fly! Fly, Phoenix!"

The bird looked at the Scientist, then at David, its glance curious but without understanding. Paralyzed with fear, David remained on his knees as the Scientist reached

an open place and threw the gun up to his shoulder. The
bullet went whining by with an ugly hornet-noise, and the
report of the gun echoed along the scarp.

"Fly, Phoenix!" David sobbed. A second bullet
snarled at the bird, and spattered out little chips of rock
from the inner wall of the ledge.

"Oh, fly, fly!" David jumped up and flung himself

between the bird and the Scientist. "It's me!" he cried. "It's David!" The bird gazed at him closely, and a light flickered in its eye as though the name had reached out and almost, but not quite, touched an ancient memory. Hesitantly it stretched forth one wing, and with the tip of it lightly brushed David's forehead, leaving there a mark that burned coolly.

"Get away from that bird, you little idiot!" the Scientist shrieked. *"GET AWAY!"*

David ignored him. "Fly, Phoenix!" he cried, and he pushed the bird toward the edge.

Understanding dawned in the amber eyes at last. The bird, with one clear, defiant cry, leaped to an outjutting boulder. The golden wings spread, the golden neck curved back, the golden talons pushed against the rock. The bird launched itself into the air and soared out over the valley, sparkling, flashing, shimmering; a flame, large as a sunburst, a meteor, a diamond, a star, diminishing at last to a speck of gold dust, which glimmered twice in the distance before it was gone altogether.

The Author

Edward Ormondroyd

When Edward Ormondroyd was about thirteen, his family moved from Pennsylvania to Ann Arbor, Michigan. He and a friend began to read Arthur Ransome's boating stories and, inspired by the adventures of the Swallows, built their own fourteen-foot sailboat and tried to re-create that English magic on the Huron River.

In 1943 he graduated from high school and joined the Navy. Destroyer Escort 419 was his home for the next two years. "When the war was over, she looked in on China and Korea, and came home. She did show me San Francisco Bay at dusk. One look convinced me that I would like to live by it; and I have, ever since."

After the war, Mr. Ormondroyd went to the University of California at Berkeley. He graduated in 1951, and since then has been busy writing, sailing as able seaman aboard a tanker, and working as a bookstore clerk and machine tender. He lives in Berkeley, California. He is married and has one son.

It was while Mr. Ormondroyd was at college that David and the Phoenix first intruded into his consciousness. *"One day, when I was walking across campus, I had a sudden vision of a large and pompous bird diving out of a window, tripping on the sill, and falling into a rose arbor below. I had to explain to myself why the poor bird was in such a situation in the first place, and what became of it afterwards. The result of my investigation was* DAVID AND THE PHOENIX."

Gupta has been published in a variety of scientific journals and has received numerous accolades. He received the health communication achievement award from the American Medical Association in 2009 and his health reports swept all three health and medical awards in 2006— the first year the National Headliner Awards honored such journalism in a dedicated category. Also in 2006, he earned his first Emmy®, a Peabody, and the DuPont award.

In 2004, the Atlanta Press Club named Gupta "Journalist of the Year." He has won the Humanitarian Award from the National Press Photographers Association, a GOLD Award from the National Health Care Communicators, and the International Health and Medical Media award known as the "Freddie." His first book, *Chasing Life*, became a *New York Times* best seller and was also the subject of a one-hour documentary of the same name on CNN.

A board-certified neurosurgeon, Gupta is a member of several organizations, including the American Association of Neurological Surgeons, Congress of Neurological Surgeons, and the Council of Foreign Relations. He serves as a diplomat of the American Board of Neurosurgery as a Fellow in the American College of Surgery and is a certified medical investigator. Gupta is also a board member of the Lance Armstrong LiveStrong Foundation.

About the Author

SANJAY GUPTA, MD, is a practicing neurosurgeon and associate chief of neurosurgery at Grady Memorial Hospital and assistant professor at Emory University Hospital in Atlanta. He is a columnist for *Time* magazine and chief medical correspondent at CNN, where he plays an integral role in the network's medical coverage, including daily reports, the show *House Call with Dr. Sanjay Gupta,* and coverage of breaking medical news. He is featured in a weekly podcast on health issues called "Paging Dr. Gupta" and writes health news stories for CNN.com and CNNHealth.com. He is also a contributor to *60 Minutes* and the *Evening News with Katie Couric* on CBS.

Before joining CNN, Gupta was a neurosurgeon at the University of Tennessee's Semmes-Murphy clinic, and before that, at the University of Michigan Medical Center. He became partner of the Great Lakes Brain and Spine Institute in 2000 and in 1997 he was chosen as a White House Fellow, one of only fifteen fellows appointed. He served as special adviser to former first lady Hillary Rodham Clinton.